One-Track Mind

One-Track Mind

A Commissioner Kary Turnell Mystery

Mark Okrant

PLAIDSWEDE PUBLISHING
Concord, New Hampshire

Printed in the United States of America

ISBN: 978-1-7-333556-8-1

Library of Congress Control Number: 2019948776

Published by:
Plaidswede Publishing
P.O. Box 269 Concord, New Hampshire 03302-0269

www.plaidswede.com

Books by Mark Okrant

Judson's Island

A Last Resort

I Knew You When

An Icy Reception

Murder with a View

Sleeping Alongside the Road:
Recollections by Patrons and Owners of Motels

No Vacancy:
The Rise, Demise, and Reprise of America's Motels

Murder at the Grands

Whacked

Death by Lobster

Two If by Sea

Acknowledgements

This first volume of the Commissioner Kary Turnell Mystery Series has been made possible by the support of a number of people. Dr. David "Lou" Ferland, retired chief of police with the Portsmouth (N.H.) Police Department, is my go-to guy on matters pertaining to crime scene investigation. Rebecca Metcalf, marketing director for the Mount Washington Cog Railway, made it possible for me to receive an insider's experience of the awe-inspiring reality provided by the Northeast's highest mountain and its fabulous, gravity-defying rail system. General manager of the Mount Washington Summit Road Company, Howie Wemyss, and his associate Crispin Battles, provided valuable information about the historic auto road and welcome center. Paul Freitas, Plymouth (N.H.) town administrator, proved to be an invaluable source of information about drug trafficking and enforcement in the White Mountains Region. Marla Okrant, my wife of nearly forty-nine years—as always—served as principal first-round editor, adviser on characters' names, and creator of the book's title. I truly could not write this series without her multi-faceted input. Robyn Okrant, the older of my two amazingly talented daughters, designed the beautiful cover for One Track Mind. Finally, the author wishes to thank George Geers,

owner of Plaidswede Publishing, for years of encourage-
ment, patience and friendship.

Foreword

When Kary returned home to New Hampshire from Ocean Beach Park, New London, Conn., not unexpectedly, he found a different Nya Turnell waiting for him. Nya deeply loved her husband. It was because of her feelings for Kary that she knew the time had come to give him an ultimatum.

"Kary, you are nearly seventy years old. For the third time in two years, you came within an eyelash of being taken away from me. You know very well that I waited a long time for you to become the husband I needed all of these years. I'm not willing to go through anything like this... ever again." She began to sob as she finished.

Kary knew Nya was right. Also, the incident with Meirs in Connecticut convinced him that this was a good time to leave private investigating. His problem was how to make use of his newly found leisure without putting himself in further danger.

"I suppose I could find a hobby," he told Nya.

The answer came in the form of a well-timed telephone call. Nya considered allowing the house phone to ring. Reluctantly, she picked up the receiver. At first, she felt that the caller was a prankster. However, after some convincing by the staffer on the other end of the line, she handed the telephone to Kary.

The caller was David Steele, newly elected governor of New Hampshire. Steele came right to the point.

"Kary…is it all right if I call you by your first name?"

"Certainly, Governor."

"I've been concerned about the growing number of incidents taking place in some of New Hampshire's state parks and tourism attractions. Tourism is far too important to this state. We need to protect our good name."

Steele sounded angry when he added, "Our rival states must be reveling in the recent incident up north."

"How can I help you, sir?" Kary inquired.

"I'm glad you asked, Kary. I want to create a new task force on visitor safety that focuses on violent crimes to persons in public spaces. Granite Staters and our out-of-state guests need to feel safe when they're enjoying New Hampshire. The task force will be comprised of state and local police and legal people from the attorney general's office. It will be part of the DOJ's Homicide Prosecution Unit, but will focus on human targets that are most vulnerable… and, frankly…produce the most negative publicity." The governor paused to allow Kary to absorb what he had just said.

"Governor, I presume you're not hiring me to make hotels and popular destinations safer."

Kary's comment made Governor Steele chuckle. "Isn't that precisely what you've been doing for the past ten years, Kary?"

Now it was Kary who was compelled to smile. "Yes, I suppose that's true."

"Then why not formalize things? I'd like to appoint you as Commissioner of the Task Force for Visitor Safety. If you accept, your appointment will become official at the beginning of the new fiscal year. The name of the task force may sound benign; but I will count on all of you to deliver protection to our visitors. I'm expecting its creation to send a clear message to perpetrators: if you cross the line, you'll be caught, prosecuted and punished swiftly and efficiently.

The governor continued. "There are two caveats, Kary. First, you'll have to promise never to put yourself in physical contact with perpetrators again. That will be the job of law enforcement personnel."

Kary smiled. "That will make my wife Nya very happy. But what's the second caveat?" he asked.

"I'll need your answer by one week from today."

When the governor hung up the phone, Kary turned to Nya and said, "I think I've just found that new hobby."

Chapter 1

It was a surprisingly warm mid-June morning at the base station of Mt. Washington's Cog Railway. For septuagenarian Arnold Dean, this was to be a special day. In several hours, he would ride the cog to the 6,288-foot summit, thereby checking one more item off his bucket list. A lifelong steam train enthusiast, Dean had booked his ticket online a month in advance. Unable to sleep the night before his trip, he drove through the night from Boston, completing the six-mile winding stretch along Base Road just before daybreak.

Dean arrived at the Cog Base Station's parking lot several hours before the Agiocochook, the vintage coal-fired locomotive, would steam up to the long platform to take on passengers. So, he slept in his car before retrieving the $75 ticket at the counter on the lower floor of the base station.

At 7:45 a.m., the moment Dean had long anticipated was only fifteen minutes from fruition. As he stood within yards of the Agiocochook, telling a group of nearby passengers how excited he was to be taking this trip, Dean removed the ticket from the pocket of his parka, then kissed it.

Standing back from the line of passengers, a man wearing a gray parka with a matching backpack and a navy blue baseball cap was watching Dean's every movement. The man in the parka knew the first train of the day—the only one that would be pushed up the mountain with a steam engine—was sold out. A taciturn man with a penchant for violent behavior, he needed to be in that first coach of the day, as a small fortune depended on it.

Moments before there was an announcement for passengers to line up, a life-changing circumstance for both men occurred. It began when Dean felt a familiar urging from his lower digestive track.

"Damned blithery Ds," he announced out loud to no one in particular. Unfortunately, for many years, Dean lived with an affliction shared by many; it was a condition that doctors had diagnosed as a nervous bowel. Not wanting to spoil the one-hour trip to the summit, Dean decided to quickly use the restroom before boarding. Despite being nearly seventy-five, Dean showed amazing quickness as he made his way into the lower level of the base station. Jostling past customers in the crowded retail store, he climbed the long wooden staircase leading to the men's room situated just outside the snack bar on the second level.

As he entered the men's room, Dean was met by the one thing he most dreaded—the single toilet stall was occupied by a man and his child.

Fearing he would miss the only steam train of the day, Dean called out, "The first train is boarding. Better hurry along."

"Thanks," came a man's reply. "We're just finishing up here."

A minute later, a tall, balding, man of about thirty and

his toddler son emerged from the stall. The father apologized to Dean, then ushered his son out of the bathroom without either washing his hands.

"Philistines!" Dean called after them, as he entered the stall. In their haste to catch the train, the boy's father had failed to wipe a stain from the toilet seat, and hadn't bothered to flush.

Dean's urgency was too great to ignore. He quickly removed his parka, then wiped away an offending trace of excrement from the seat, flushed the toilet, and papered the seat. As he sat down, the precious cog ticket fell from the pocket of his parka onto the floor and slid just out of reach.

At that moment, Dean heard the men's room door open, and observed a pair of hiking boots near the spot where his ticket had slid under the stall door. Seconds later, a hand appeared and snatched up the ticket. Expecting the intruder to slide his ticket back into the stall, Dean sat in grateful silence. To his horror, he saw the feet turn toward the bathroom door.

Springing to his feet without pulling up his jeans, Dean opened the door and was prepared to verbally confront the intruder. He did not have the chance. Knowing that passengers for the first train of the day were already outside on the loading platform, the intruder acted instinctively. He grabbed Dean by the throat with his left hand. With his right hand, he punched Dean twice, crushing the old man's larynx. With Dean incapacitated and the Agiocochook's whistle sounding on the track below, the intruder sat the old man's motionless body back down on the toilet. He retrieved Dean's glasses from the men's room floor and, holding onto the lenses, slid them onto his face. Then, without so much as a look over his shoulder, the intruder headed downstairs, and out a door leading to the platform. The man in gray felt no remorse.

The steam engine sat waiting to push a single, bright orange coach up the cog railway. The intruder quickly apologized to the young woman staff member for his tardiness. After handing her his stolen ticket to be scanned, he climbed aboard the coach and took the one remaining seat.

Chapter 2

By 8:00 that same morning, Ned Garett was just arriving at the headquarters of the Mt. Washington Auto Road, situated at the base of the east flank of Mt. Washington in Glen. Garrett, a tall, dark-haired, thirty-year old unemployed maintenance worker, guided his white Chevy Malibu up the steep drive leading to the Mt. Washington Stage Lines. Before parking his car, Garrett peered at the large, two-story clapboard structure. The rectangular sign above the door read, 'Welcome – Bienvenue.' Having made the trip south from Quebec City many times during the past months, he smiled at the notion of being welcomed to New Hampshire, for Ned Garrett was not traveling on vacation.

Garrett was the sort of person who was easy to like. He had a certain natural charm that was completely at odds with his current profession—as a drug mule for a fledgling cartel.

"If they only knew why I'm riding to the summit." Garrett couldn't resist smiling at his employers' latest scheme to avoid capture by federal and state officials.

For months, law enforcement was laboring to prevent his network from completing its chosen task: to move drugs—marijuana, cocaine and opiates—along the pipeline between Canada and markets in northern New England.

Garrett backed his Chevy Malibu into a preselected parking space. Before exiting his car, Garrett reached into the glove box and removed his Quebec registration. He then opened the trunk, removed a gray parka and matching backpack. Before crossing the large paved lot and heading toward the main entrance of the building, Garrett placed his car keys in a small zippered pocket at the front of the pack.

A circular sign above the entryway announced this as the headquarters of the Mt. Washington Auto Road. His employers had been methodical about what Garrett was to do and what to avoid. He was to walk through the green double-steel doors and purchase a Stage ticket. Situated immediately inside the entranceway, the ticket window was easy to spot. As he'd been instructed, a brown sign lettered 'Stage Fares' was positioned strategically over the window.

A diminutive, white-haired woman dressed in blue jeans and a checkered flannel shirt approached the window from the administrative office situated behind it.

"What can I do you for, sir?" she asked.

"I'd like to take a ride to the top," Garrett replied, while suppressing his natural urge to converse with the woman.

"Well then, you're in the right place," she replied with a smile. "One way or round trip?"

Garrett looked up at the signboard, pretending to be indecisive. He already knew that the price of a round-trip ticket would be $30. In fact, he had prepared himself in advance by placing that exact amount, three $10 bills, in his jeans pocket. Garrett deliberately kept the conversation short. "I'll go round trip," he told her.

"Most folks do. Besides, you're not dressed for hiking," she replied.

It made Garrett uncomfortable that the old woman had noted his attire. His employers were adamant that its drug traffickers not draw attention to themselves. Law enforcement hadn't caught them thus far; but there was no sense in pushing their luck. Garrett shrugged. He was good at what he did, especially staying below the cops' radar. Of course, the cartel's continued success depended on the other carriers being similarly careful.

"Will I be able to get onto the first stage?" he asked.

"You're in luck, young man," she replied. "We expected a group of hikers here this morning, but they haven't arrived. More important for you, they haven't paid for their tickets."

Not wanting to draw any further attention to himself, Garrett nodded his thanks and headed farther into the Stage's welcome center. First, he went into the retail store and immediately saw the item he needed to buy. Minutes later, he exited the store wearing a navy blue baseball cap with Mt. Washington Auto Road printed on the front. Before heading out to the van, Garrett entered the large wood-paneled canteen where he purchased a pastry and a cup of strong coffee to go.

Chapter 3

One hundred and twenty-five miles to the south, the mood in the offices of New Hampshire's Drug Task Force was anything but jubilant. Administered by the state attorney general's office, the DTF was comprised of investigators from the attorney general's office and officers from local, county and state police departments. Since 1986, federal funds had underwritten the affairs of the agency.

At 33 Capitol St., in downtown Concord, on the second floor of a large former bank building, a meeting of the DTF was in progress in the conference room. At the head of the large oval oak table sat Bill Williams, director of DTF. Williams, a stern forty year-old former college football defensive tackle, looked less happy than usual. Slapping his meaty open hand on the table, the director brought the meeting to order.

"Gentlemen and ladies," he began, "we are losing this damned war on drugs. A week ago, I thought we were making some progress. But, all of a sudden, there seem to be more illegal drugs in the north country than ever." Looking around the table, he said, "Someone tell me something positive."

Lieutenant Mary Bendix, a career law enforcement officer was in the last year of her three-year term on the

DTF. Bendix was in her early fifties. Trim to the point of appearing waif-like, she had clawed her way through the old boy network, finally earning her officer's bars at the age of forty-eight.

It was Bendix who spoke first. "As some of you know, we're onto a guy named Ned Garrett, who's working out of Quebec City," she offered.

This was the first DTF meeting for young Bob Norton. Sergeant Norton was a couple of inches shorter than six feet with a muscular physique and forearms the size of most men's calves. Norton had been assigned to the DTF recently by his Claremont police department. A few years shy of thirty, Norton was already a highly decorated police officer who carried a reputation for questioning authority. Impatient to stake his place at the table, Norton committed the sin of challenging a fellow task force member.

Fixing his steely blue eyes on Bendix, he demanded, "If you're onto this guy Garrett, why the heck is he still on the street?"

Bendix was quick to respond. Not intimidated by Norton's physical presence nor his reputation as a rising hotshot in law enforcement, she looked him directly in the eyes and replied, "Since you're new here and aren't familiar with protocol, I'll forgive the tone of your comment, Sergeant. However, I'm embarrassed for you that the answer to that question is patently obvious."

Before Norton could respond, Williams cleared his throat. Speaking softly, he looked at the young male officer and replied, "We wouldn't accomplish a damned thing by pulling in Garrett. Arresting one player isn't going to take drugs off the streets for long. He'd just be replaced by another mule. What Officer Bendix was about to say is we need to keep our eyes on Garrett. If we can confirm his connection with the cartel, we may be able to use him to bag the entire Quebec operation."

Norton realized his error and immediately apologized to Bendix and the rest of the group.

"No offense taken, Sergeant," she replied. "We need people who give a damn on this task force. Your energy will prove helpful in the long run." Then, with a sardonic grin, she added, "Within certain limits, of course."

Williams informed the group, "We're watching Garrett. Fortunately for us, he's not quite as smart as he thinks he is. Our man in the field tailed him from the Quebec border to the Mt. Washington Auto Road. He tells me that Garrett took a break this morning to go sightseeing."

"Sightseeing?" several around the table questioned Williams.

"Yeah, he's heading up the mountain as we speak."

※ ※ ※ ※ ※ ※

Housed in the same building was the office of the newly formed Task Force for Visitor Safety. Commissioner Kary Turnell was slowly climbing the proverbial walls. After decades as a highly regarded academic criminologist and, more recently, a well-earned reputation as a private investigator, Kary had accepted Governor Steele's offer to serve as the task force's first commissioner.

During the forty days that Kary had occupied his new position, there wasn't a single relevant incident. What there had been was a deluge of media occasions and meetings. Kary had met with everyone from the governor, to the head of human resources, to two reporters from WMUR-TV's Chronicle program, to the director of the state's Drug Task Force.

That last meeting proved to be the least pleasant. Not that Kary had a personal problem with Bill Williams. In fact, Williams reminded Kary of his old friend, Lieutenant Henry May, the state police officer who saved his life years earlier. Williams was a large, personable guy. However, the news that he shared with Kary nearly sent the newly minted commissioner into orbit.

"You were told by the governor that you'd have your own task force. Am I right, Kary?"

Kary nodded.

"That isn't gonna happen," the large man deadpanned.

Kary saw red. "What do you mean it isn't going to happen?" he bristled.

"The governor assured me I'd have my own team."

Williams laughed at Kary's naiveté about the workings of state government. "You met Jayne Ingolls, your new admin assistant, right?"

"Of course."

"Well, Kary, I'm afraid she's your entire task force," Williams informed him. "The governor is new on the block. Since he talked with you, he's had to learn the realities of budgeting with a Republican-controlled legislature."

Kary sat there fuming.

"Not to worry," Williams attempted to lighten his new colleague's mood.

"Why shouldn't I worry? The governor assured me when I took this job that I'd have a highly qualified team of investigators and litigators to support any necessary actions." Remembering his wife Nya's concern about several close calls at the hands of perpetrators he'd been chasing during the last several years, Kary asked Williams a sarcastic question.

"What am I supposed to do, strap on a gun?"

Williams respected Kary, so he suppressed a smile with difficulty.

"No, you won't need to do that. My investigators will be your investigators and my litigators will be your litigators," the DTF director replied. "We'll make this work until you get more clout in the capitol building."

Chapter 4

The intruder occupied an aisle seat three rows from the front of the orange Cog Railway coach. Within moments after he sat down, the steam-powered engine propelled the coach forward with a jerk, and the long, steep climb began. The intruder made no effort at eye contact with the young couple sitting next to him. They couldn't know how close they were to a man who, mere minutes before, took the life of an innocent tourist.

The intruder was a man on a mission. Unlike others inside the coach who marveled at the magnificent scenery on the Northeast's tallest mountain, he concentrated on what awaited him at the summit. He knew that, upon disembarking, he would be looking for a man he did not know personally, but whose appearance should be unmistakable.

As the small train continued its sharp climb, the brakeman on board announced that they were approaching the Waumbek tank, a large steel structure on stilts designed to provide one thousand gallons of water when the engine needed it.

The intruder looked at his watch. He was on a tight schedule and was nervous that a stop to take on water would make him late for his rendezvous at the summit. The cartel had told him that the other drug carrier would wait only ten minutes, then depart. To the intruder's relief, the brakeman announced that the engine would not be taking on water until a later run.

The coach passed the Halfway House, a small shelter that looked like it might slide down the mountain at any moment. As if the brakeman read the intruder's mind, he announced that the appearance of the building was an optical illusion. It was actually sitting on the level, whereas those aboard the coach were climbing on a considerable angle.

In spite of his preoccupation with the task ahead of him, the intruder was impressed as the train entered Jacob's Ladder, a trestle whose thirty-seven degree grade made this the steepest part of the climb. Looking out the window, the intruder spotted two deep ravines, which the brakeman identified as Ammonoosuc and Burt's. Next, pointing toward the horizon above them, the brakeman identified three mile-high peaks: mounts Adams, Jefferson and Clay.

Just as the summit appeared in the distance, the brakeman directed the passengers' attention to the Lizzie Bourne marker. It was a large stone feature that showed the site where a solo woman climber perished after prolonged exposure to the elements. The irony of the Bourne story was that she died a short distance below the summit, where help awaited.

Momentarily disregarding his employers' instructions, the intruder turned his head toward the couple sitting next to him and spoke loud enough for them to hear.

"Terrible way to go," he muttered in their direction, a direct contradiction of the cartel's orders.

At 9:05, the engine and coach came to a stop next to a concrete platform, where the passengers disembarked. The intruder's real task was just beginning.

※ ※ ※ ※ ※ ※

Ned Garrett occupied the one remaining seat in the fifteen-passenger Mt. Washington Stage Line van. With all seats filled, the van pulled out of the parking lot several minutes before its 8:30 scheduled departure time. Negotiating the steep auto road, with its numerous sudden curves and enormous rises, necessitated driving skills and careful attention to treacherous conditions. Garrett was interested in learning more about the training that had been required of the driver, Julie Mathews. His personal interest in Julie, a comely redhead, was even greater. However, his instructions had been quite clear. Don't engage anyone: not at the base, in the stage, nor at the summit. This way, witnesses would be less likely to remember him, in case he was arrested. Garrett knew he'd said too much to the older woman at the ticket window, earlier. "What the hell," he told himself, "who's going to believe an old lady, anyway?"

As the stage climbed up the auto road, Julie pointed out a number of interesting geological and vegetation features. Garrett was interested in geography since he was a boy and marveled at the notion that the passengers could see examples of almost every global vegetation zone just by climbing the steep 7.6-mile road.

When the van arrived at the summit just before 9:00, Garrett looked for black smoke coming from the steam engine. The atmosphere at the top of the mountain was remarkably clear. Garrett peered into the distance at the exact moment that a large plume appeared just below the ridge where he was standing. Realizing that he still had several minutes before his contact arrived, Garrett entered the Sherman Adams Summit Building and went in search of a men's room. After relieving himself, Garrett walked back to the entryway, where he stood and awaited the arrival of the stranger he would be meeting.

Chapter 5

When the steam engine came to a full stop, the intruder left the train. In his haste to leave, he completely ignored the first two rows of passengers, offering no apology. The young couple that had been seated next to the intruder simply looked at other passengers and shrugged.

"He's not with us," the husband offered.

The intruder bolted up the hill and entered the Sherman Adams building, feigning desperation to use the men's room. In truth, his sole purpose was to determine whether his contact was still in the building. As the intruder entered the two-story concrete-and-glass structure, Ned Garrett was standing just inside the doorway.

As the intruder passed, Garrett immediately recognized that this was his contact. How could he not? Each man was wearing a gray Swiss Army parka with a matching Swissgear backpack. Both men were dressed in blue jeans. The one item of clothing that defined each of them was a baseball cap from the respective modes of transportation. The intruder wore a navy blue Cog Railway cap, while Garrett's navy baseball cap read Mt. Washington Auto Road.

As had been prearranged, the intruder made no eye contact with Garrett. He used the men's room, then walked downstairs to the Extreme Mt. Washington Museum, the interactive facility that was designed to give summer visitors a sense of winter on the summit. The intruder walked throughout the exhibits, frequently jostling others in the crowd as he went. He never stopped to look at anything, and made certain not to interact with anyone.

By design, ten minutes had passed since the intruder walked past Ned Garrett. At precisely 9:25, the intruder again passed Garrett, this time heading out the Adams Building's main entrance. Garrett counted slowly to fifty, then exited as well. By the time Garrett was outside, he could see the intruder about to enter the Tip Top House, the historic lodge standing on a high point of land immediately adjacent to the Adams Building. Garrett climbed the short, winding trail that led to the Tip Top House. Unlike the confederate with whom he was about to rendezvous, Garrett took a moment to appreciate the structure, whose outer walls consisted of rough-cut granite rock.

When Garrett entered the old structure, he found himself viewing a re-creation of a mid-nineteenth century lobby, complete with a front desk and large, iron potbelly stove.

The intruder was nowhere to be seen, so Garrett moved past the front desk into a second room. This one was set up as a dining room, with eight chairs surrounding a large round table, and place-settings for the same number of guests.

"Where the hell is that guy?" Garrett muttered.

Garrett doubled back down a parallel corridor. The cartel had prepared him for what was to happen. Inside there were three sets of bunk beds, each designed to sleep three persons. Garrett noticed that the curtains for the first set of beds had been drawn closed. He waited for a single straggler to leave the bunkroom, then removed his backpack and baseball cap. Pulling back the curtain, Garrett spotted a backpack identical to his own and a Cog Railway baseball cap. Garrett placed his backpack and baseball cap on the same wooden platform, donned the intruder's items, then closed the curtain on the bunk bed.

Garrett walked slowly back through the lobby and the dining room. When he reentered the sleeping quarters a minute later, he pulled back the curtain on the bunk bed. His backpack and cap were gone.

Chapter 6

Kary Turnell sat with his feet propped up on the wooden desk provided by the governor's office. As he basked in a beam of early morning sunlight, his thoughts turned to his daughter, Sara, who was pregnant with the grandchild Nya and he had long desired. Without warning, Kary was jolted upright by the buzz of his office intercom. Jayne Ingolls, his mid-fifties administrative assistant, was on the line.

"What can I do for you, Jayne?" Kary yawned. "Let me guess, the governor wants me to have lunch with a diplomat from Papua New Guinea."

Jayne replied without missing a beat, "I'd heard you have amazing powers of deduction, Commissioner. I'm really disappointed," she deadpanned.

Kary laughed at his admin's repartee.

"Since I was slightly off the mark with my last effort, perhaps it will be best if you just tell me the real reason for your call."

"Simone Fletcher from DTF just phoned. Apparently Mr. Williams wants to see you in the DTF conference room ASAP."

Kary was bewildered by Williams' urgent request. It was apparent that the DTF director wasn't asking him to meet simply to be cordial. So, he stood up, walked into the outer office and instructed Ingolls, "Wish me luck," before heading down the hall to DTF's suite of offices.

Kary opened the door without knocking. He was greeted by Simone Fletcher, the longtime administrative assistant for that agency. Fletcher had met Kary at one of his many meetings, and the pair immediately clicked. Fletcher greeted Kary with a broad smile and a firm handshake.

"Good afternoon, Commissioner Turnell."

Despite being in his post for more than a month, Kary was still not accustomed to being addressed as 'Commissioner.'

"Do you have any idea why Bill Williams wants to see me so urgently?"

"That information is way above my pay grade, Commissioner," she replied. "However, after forty years working for these characters, I've become pretty good at reading between the lines."

"And what, pray tell, is your reading telling you at this moment?"

"I'd say a certain brand new commissioner is about to become very busy," she winked.

At 8:30, when Kary entered the conference room, he didn't expect to be greeted by nearly a dozen people. Seeing Kary's puzzled expression, Williams smiled broadly, "I need to remember to have Simone invite you to our next card game."

"Is my poker face that bad?" Kary asked.

"The worst," Williams replied while pointing to a vacant chair at the conference table, situated directly opposite from where the DTF director was seated.

As Kary sat, Williams said to the group, "Some of you already met Dr. Kary Turnell, our new Commissioner for Visitor Safety. We'll work on formal introductions to everyone else later on. For now, I want you to get familiar with two people, Kary."

Williams nodded toward a middle-age woman seated next to him. "This is Lieutenant Mary Bendix. Mary's bio is in the top folder sitting on the table in front of you."

Williams continued, "To your immediate left is Sergeant Bob Norton. His file is also in front of you. However, you should know that Lieutenant Bendix is a first-rate criminologist and a whiz at digging up the most obscure material off the Internet. As for Sergeant Norton, once you've read his file, Nya and you will sleep better at night." Williams was aware that Kary's wife Nya was deeply concerned about his safety, especially following several close calls during the past several years.

"Let's just say, if you locked the sergeant in a room with the Green Bay Packers, I'd give even odds about who would emerge."

Kary looked over at the two officers. Bendix appeared unfazed by Williams' comments, while Norton looked uncomfortable to be singled out in front of the entire task force.

Before Kary could say anything, Bendix focused her steel gray eyes on him. "It will be a pleasure working with you, Commissioner. Everyone in this room is familiar with what you bring to the table," she added without any trace of a smile. Bendix was being sincere. As the new commissioner would soon learn, she was all business, and not about to waste her time patronizing him, or anyone else, for that matter.

Kary nodded his thanks to the assembled. Then, sensing there was some source of tension in the room, he told everyone, "I'm honored to be among so many outstanding law enforcement officials, but will someone please tell me what is going on!"

Kary's comment proved to be a well-needed tension buster. After everyone enjoyed a hearty laugh, Williams quickly reestablished control of the room.

"Kary, we've been contacted by the Major Crime Unit. Apparently, there's been an incident at the Cog Railway Base Station. We think it may be related to a drug smuggling operation we've been investigating for several months.

Kary was momentarily puzzled. Looking around the room once again, he said to no one in particular, "Drug control is DTF's bailiwick. How does this concern Visitor Safety?"

Not one to refrain from bringing up sensitive topics, it was Sergeant Norton who replied, "There's a dead tourist in the men's room at the Cog, Commissioner."

Chapter 7

It was 9:35 when Garrett reemerged from the Tip Top House. He saw the familiar gray parka, backpack and navy blue cap moving down a path a hundred yards away. The intruder was making his way toward the parking lot where, less than thirty minutes earlier, Garrett had disembarked from the Mt. Washington Stage Line van. Since everything was going according to their bosses' plans, Garrett headed toward the Cog's passenger platform.

Once aboard the same orange cog railway coach that had carried the intruder to the summit, Garrett sat in the second row of seats. By coincidence, the couple that earlier sat next to the intruder was now sitting across the aisle from him. Garrett barely took notice when the young woman's expression changed from a look of recognition to a visage reflecting her confusion.

❊ ❊ ❊ ❊ ❊ ❊

As the cog coach descended the mountain, Garrett allowed himself to relax a bit and enjoyed his first view of the landscape on the west slope of Mt. Washington. However, he purposefully didn't participate when his fellow passengers waved at each diesel engine that pushed a colorful coach up the steep mountain.

As the steam engine and coach descended farther and farther, Garrett became more and more impressed with the nineteenth-century cog system. When the coach was several miles down the mountain, he could see the red roof and white outer walls of the Omni Mt. Washington Hotel in the distance. Amazingly, it appeared that the grand hotel occupied an elevation even higher than the one where Garrett and his fellow passengers were situated. However, the brakeman informed them that, once again, they were experiencing an optical illusion. Twenty minutes later, when the base station came into view, Garrett became aware of a great deal of activity on the passenger platform a quarter of a mile below. Something else about the situation confused him. Beyond the station, in the roadway and parking lot, sat what appeared to be a cavalcade of police cars—their blue lights aglow.

By the time the coach came to a full stop, it was 10:15. Garrett had an irresistible craving for a cup of coffee. However, when he exited the coach and attempted to enter the base station, Garrett was stopped by a state police officer.

"Where are you headed, sir?" the officer asked him.

Garrett considered himself to be an old hand at talking to law enforcement officials, so he kept his cool.

"I just need cup of coffee, officer. Then I'm headed out to my car and back to Canada," he replied. Garrett immediately wondered whether he'd been wise to say anything about his destination. However, the officer did not seem to take special notice.

"I'm afraid the base station is temporarily closed, sir. You'll need to stop someplace down the road for that."

Garrett grew bold, bolder than his bosses would have appreciated.

"May I ask why the base station is closed?" he asked the officer.

"Let's just say there's been an incident and leave it at that. If you want further information, I can introduce you to my lieutenant over there," he replied while pointing to a tall uniformed state trooper who was interviewing employees just outside the main entrance.

Garrett wanted no part of that. As an experienced drug mule, the last thing Garrett wanted to do was call attention to himself. And, that is precisely what he had just done.

Things didn't get any better when Garrett began to search for the car that the intruder had left in the parking lot. The bosses' orders for the intruder were to leave his car reasonably close to the base station, but not so close that entry into the vehicle would attract the curiosity of others. Garrett's first attempt to spot the white Chevy Malibu—a twin of the car he had parked on the other side of the mountain—was proving fruitless. Making matters difficult, the parking lot was nearly full.

As he searched, Garrett was reminded of a childhood episode, specifically of a time when he became separated from his mother at the grand opening of a neighborhood supermarket. On that occasion, Garrett had cried aloud and kept on crying, until a store clerk helped him find his mother. How he wished things were that simple now.

As Garrett searched for the Malibu, he heard a familiar voice behind him.

"Are you having a problem, sir?" It was the same officer with whom he'd just talked.

At that very moment, he spotted the Malibu near the east end of the parking lot, in the farthest corner away from the base station.

"That stupid mother F'er," Garrett exclaimed aloud.

"Did you say something?" the officer asked.

"Oh, no, officer. I was just calling myself names for forgetting where I put my car this morning."

When the officer headed back to the base station to join the other state troopers, Garrett figured he had dodged a bullet. Seeing that the officer was far enough in the distance, Garrett reached into the backpack he had swapped with the intruder inside the Tip Top House and retrieved a set of Chevy Malibu keys. To a casual observer, the car's trunk appeared to be empty, save for a spare tire with a magnetic license plate partially wedged beneath it. Garrett quickly checked to see that the number on the plate was the same as the one on the car he'd left in the Stage parking lot. The match was perfect. Garrett promptly slapped this magnetic Quebec province license plate over the one from Massachusetts that was mounted to the back of the intruder's Malibu. Next, he hid the contents of the backpack, employing the method all of the cartel's carriers had been instructed to use.

Garrett hoped to leave the area immediately but that

was not going to happen. All cars exiting the lot were required to line up, so the drivers and their passengers could be interviewed. When he saw that the same officer he'd just talked with was conducting the interviews, Garrett began to perspire.

"I'll bet that you're still craving that cup of Joe," the officer teased him.

"Yes. It's been hours since my last coffee."

"I know the feeling, sir. I promise that we won't be keeping you very long. Just show me your license and registration."

Garrett handed the officer his license and the registration he'd brought from the car parked in the Stage lot. After five minutes had passed, Garrett began to be concerned.

"What the heck is taking that damned cop so long to come back?"

After an additional few minutes passed, Garrett tried to convince himself not to worry. "My bosses have thought of nearly everything, from the identical white Malibus, to similar gray clothing and backpacks, to the license plates and switched registrations."

As he sat there waiting for the officer to return, Garrett suddenly realized that there was one huge stumbling block: the two cars had different vehicle identification numbers, or VINs.

It seemed to Garrett that the officer was spending longer with his license and registration than he had with the driver ahead of him in line.

"Why is that damned officer talking to his lieutenant?" Garrett muttered, "If they check the VIN on this car, I'm screwed."

To Garrett's relief, the officer returned to the line of cars and handed him his documents, apparently without bothering to match the VIN on his registration to the one on this car.

"What took so long?" Garrett asked. "Was something wrong?"

"Nothing to worry about, sir. My lieutenant just wanted to adjust the lunch schedule."

Garrett didn't know if he could believe the story about lunch schedules. But, one thing was for certain, he was heading back to Quebec City without delay.

As Garrett headed down the Base Road, he asked himself, "What the hell did that other idiot do inside the Base Station this morning?"

※ ※ ※ ※ ※ ※

The intruder's trip down the mountain was less eventful, albeit more time-consuming than Garrett's had been. On two occasions, the brake lights in the van had illuminated. Each time, the driver pulled into a lookout on the side of the steep, winding road and waited. When she did this, the driver was quick to explain that there was nothing wrong, but a ten-minute wait was necessitated in order to allow the brake pads to cool. By the time the van returned to the base station in Glen, the intruder was nearly one-half-hour behind schedule and in a foul mood.

Despite the delay, the intruder was in a better position to complete his part of the plan than Garrett found himself earlier. The reason for this was simple. Garrett had followed orders to the letter that morning. He avoided any memorable interactions, placed his white Chevy Malibu in an easily located parking spot, and—most important—Garrett hadn't murdered anyone.

Just as Garrett had done when he arrived at the Cog parking lot,

the intruder opened the trunk at the Stage lot with the car key that was left in the backpack the pair had exchanged in the Tip Top House. The intruder stowed the his backpack in the trunk, then removed a magnetic Massachusetts license plate from beneath the spare tire. As Garrett had done thirty miles to the west, the intruder clipped the Massachusetts plate over the Quebec plate on the rear bumper of Garrett's car. However, as a neophyte in such maneuvers, the intruder was not careful enough. So, when he began to drive out of the parking space, there was a metal clanking sound, which the intruder dismissed as a wayward soda can.

Several seconds later, the intruder was startled by a knock on the car's passenger side window. A tall, heavyset man with a red beard and a complexion to match stood there signaling for the intruder to roll down his window. The intruder's initial instinct was to simply drive away, but the bearded man was adamant.

Lowering the window, the intruder took a deep breath, forcing himself not to lose his cool. There had already been enough of that for one day.

"What do you need, mister?" he asked, a bit too gruffly.

"Your license plate," the man replied.

"What about my license plate?" the intruder asked. His patience was quickly wearing thin.

"It's on the ground beneath your car."

The intruder exited the car. Sure enough, the plate was lying face down on the ground, having bounced under the rear bumper of the Malibu. The intruder reached down and, in one motion, retrieved the plate and, this time, set it properly on top of the original plate. With the situation fixed, he walked around the car, opened the driver's side door and got back inside. With the clock on his dash showing 11:00, the intruder drove away without so much as a thank you to the bearded man.

As the Malibu exited the parking lot, the bearded man called out, "You're welcome, asshole!"

The bearded man had no idea how fortunate he'd just been. If the intruder felt the slightest suspicion that the good Samaritan saw the front of the magnetic license plate, he would have killed him on the spot.

Chapter 8

Ten minutes after Kary entered the DTF conference room, Williams broke up the meeting, asking Kary, Bendix and Norton to remain behind.

"So, Kary, how do you want to proceed?" Williams asked. The question was one part protocol and one part appraisal. As a commissioner, Kary technically outranked Williams; however, more to the point, Williams was anxious to see how Kary handled the logistics of an investigation. Would he be comfortable designing an investigative strategy on the fly? How would he use personnel who were totally unfamiliar to him?

It didn't take long for any concerns to be assuaged.

"As I see things, Bill, this isn't a solo Visitor Safety investigation. DTF and Safety will need to be on one page. It will help if you'll ask Simone to arrange the quickest possible transportation to the Cog Base Station."

Kary paused for a moment, looking at Williams and Bendix, then continued, "I don't know how your protocol works, Bill. But, I presume Lieutenant Bendix will come up to the Cog Base Station with me, while you remain here to coordinate things from this end."

Williams nodded. "If this were a DTF solo investigation, that's how I would handle it."

Kary replied. "I'm certain the lieutenant here will be a tremendous resource for both of our interests. As for the good sergeant, I'm not going anywhere without him." Kary smiled at Norton.

Bendix and Norton left the room, but not before informing Kary to meet them in the parking lot on the Capitol Street side of the building. Once the two DTF officers had closed the door, Williams said to Kary, "You're more than ready for this. And, I'm pretty sure Bendix and Norton see it the same way."

Kary replied, "There is one thing we'll need to know ASAP."

"Name it."

"We need information about the victim, and the time and cause of death."

"Some of that information is just coming in. We'll wire it to Lieutenant Bendix while you're in transit; she'll coordinate communications and field research for you. You'll have all the information that we've compiled prior to your arrival in Bretton Woods. What I can tell you is this, the victim's body was found at 8:05. A cog patron found it right after the first coach of the day left for the summit."

"Damn! That means the perpetrator, or perpetrators, could be anywhere by now."

Before heading downstairs, Kary called back to Williams, "Just for my piece of mind, is there anything you need me to know about my two colleagues?"

Williams did have something to share with Kary. "Yes.

To be candid, I'm not sure how well this pair will work together. Bendix is an old hand at DTF, but Norton is our new guy. He's an outstanding, highly decorated police officer. But, he's something of an unknown as far as this agency is concerned."

Williams continued, "Here's one thing you should know about each of them. Bendix is brilliant. Unfortunately, because of her gender, she's been passed over for a bunch of promotions she should have had long ago. I can assure you, if she feels respected, Bendix will go the extra mile for you. She has a deductive mind like yours. But, unlike you, she is a whiz with current day communications."

"Thanks, Bill. This is helpful information."

Williams considered his words about Norton carefully. "Norton is a man's man. He's macho to a fault. He gets the highest scores statewide in weapons qualification year after year. Not only that, he holds high degree black belts in at least two martial arts disciplines."

"So, what aren't you telling me, Bill?"

"Norton will need to understand who's boss out there. Once he does, you'll have an associate who commands the respect of every uniformed officer in the state."

Before they parted company, Williams offered, "Here's my recommendation. Since you don't have your own task force, you're going to need to rely on the officers in the field to do physical investigations, make arrests and that sort of thing." Williams paused as the intercom buzzed. He thanked Simone on the other end, then set the receiver down.

"You have a big advantage over some bureaucrat that the governor could have selected for your post... your reputation as a criminologist and a working investigator is impeccable."

Kary appreciated Williams compliment, but asked, "I presume you think I'll do best to have Sergeant Norton interact with the officers in the field; am I correct?"

"That's how I'd handle things," Williams answered. "Good luck out there, Kary. By the way, that message was from Simone saying your car is waiting and a chopper will be ready to take off shortly after you get to the airport."

The two men shook hands. It was barely 9:00 in the morning, and things already were off to an interesting start.

※ ※ ※ ※ ※ ※

The state police helicopter carrying Kary, Bendix and Norton was capable of comfortably cruising at slightly faster than 100 knots. The pilot informed them that their ETA would be fifty minutes after take off.

Kary looked at his watch. Seeing that it was already 0940, he appeared agitated.

Norton's voice came through the chopper's headsets. "Does flying in these things make you uneasy, Commissioner?"

Kary knew that the only way they were going to bring a killer to justice was by collecting a lot of pertinent evidence during a short period of time. If that happened, they had a reasonable chance of success. Otherwise, their odds of finding the killer would be nearly zero.

When Kary finally replied to Norton, he said, "Actually, this is my first

helicopter trip, Sergeant. But, if I seem preoccupied, it's because I'm afraid the bastard is going to get away. Not exactly a stellar start for a new commissioner, eh?"

"We can completely appreciate your motivation, Commissioner," Norton replied. Then, in his typical no-holds-barred manner, he added, "Now, take your level of concern for this single victim and multiply it times hundreds... even thousands... that's how many people these drug cartels are killing each year."

To get his attention, Bendix touched Kary on the shoulder. "Don't put a wager on your perpetrator yet, Commissioner. Bendix continued, "We learned this morning that one of the drug mules we've been watching, Ned Garrett, may be linked to this. He was spotted leaving a white Chevy Malibu in the Stage parking lot in Glen earlier this morning. "

"Glen?" Norton interrupted. "That's more than thirty road miles around the mountains from the Cog's base station."

"Exactly, Sergeant," Bendix replied. "Any thoughts about what that means, gentlemen?" she questioned while displaying a twinkle in her eye for the first time.

Kary knew that Bendix's question was not aimed at Norton. She was testing his celebrated powers of deduction. He did not disappoint.

"If your man Garrett was headed up the mountain from

Glen, and the murderer is using the Cog to reach the summit, I'd wager we have two people working together."

Norton let out a sharp whistle. "Holy crap!"

With more than twenty minutes remaining before they were scheduled to land in the parking lot of the Cog Base Station, Kary asked his two new colleagues to bring him up to speed about New Hampshire's drug wars.

Bendix, with some help from Norton, explained about drug abuse and how the drug cartels operated.

"For the last several years, the number of drug-related deaths in New Hampshire has hovered around the four hundred mark."

Kary shook his head in disbelief. "Four hundred!"

Bendix continued, "Those were the unlucky ones. Each year, local EMTs administer more than two thousand doses of the anti-overdose drug, Narcan. Emergency responses to overdoses are an ever-increasing part of our firefighters' workloads."

"I had no idea there were so many drug addicts in New Hampshire," Kary replied.

"Just so you know, Commissioner, the term 'addict' is a no-no," Norton told him. "These are people who have substance abuse disorders. It's the state's number one mental health issue."

"What we're telling you is just the tip of the iceberg," Bendix continued. "The impact goes far beyond the drug users themselves. Think about how many parents, children, other family members, employers and employees are impacted."

"Which drugs are we talking about?" Kary asked.

"Until recently, we were mainly looking at addiction to opiates and opioids, such as heroin and fentanyl," Norton replied.

"Our little state ranks number two in the nation for opioid-related deaths per capita," Bendix offered. "Sadly, we're number one in fentanyl deaths."

"I'm not familiar with fentanyl," Kary told them.

"Fentanyl is an opioid... probably fifty to a hundred times stronger than heroin. It's really our number one problem... for now."

"What do you mean, 'for now'?" Kary asked.

"Because there are other prevalent drugs... crack cocaine, methamphetamines and heroin laced with fentanyl."

At that moment, the pilot, who had been listening intently to their discussion, interrupted. "Sorry to break in, Commissioner, but we're about five minutes from touch down in the Cog's lower parking lot."

Kary thanked the pilot, then asked Bendix and Norton about the origin of drugs in the state.

"That's the interesting part," Bendix replied. "Historically, we were concerned about drugs coming into the state through Massachusetts. I-93 was the main conduit. Marijuana, cocaine and opiates originating in Mexico or Honduras arrived through cities like Lawrence. Hell, El Chapo himself was in New Hampshire to supervise a few years before he was caught. The feds, mainly ATF, have worked closely with us in DTF. We've done a reasonably effective job of stemming the flow from that direction."

"But the flow obviously continues," Kary said.

"It's a never-ending fight," Norton said. "These drugs can be shipped and distributed in small quantities because they're so potent."

"And, so valuable," Bendix added.

"How valuable?" Kary asked.

"Ten grams of heroin, or what the mules call a 'finger,' retails for more than $200, and can sell for at least 400 in rural areas of the state," she replied.

"These guys are like jackals," Norton added. "They know where the methadone clinics are located. So, they camp outside and tempt recovering patients with their poison."

Just before their helicopter was about to land, Kary asked Bendix and Norton how this fellow Garrett fit into the cartels they'd just been describing.

"He's working for a new cartel, not the one that brings drugs across the border from Massachusetts," Bendix said. "There's a cartel working in the northern part of New Hampshire; and Garrett is one of their key mules. He brings drugs down from somewhere in Quebec, probably Quebec City, which has an important international airport and seaport. We're pretty sure that's where he gets his supply. Until recently, he's been meeting with someone in the stretch between Berlin and Wolfeboro. We figure they go to some pre-arranged parking lot or bar, exchange drugs for money, and Garrett returns home with the cash. We've been tracking Garrett for a couple of months."

Kary asked, "Then why haven't you picked him up?"

Recalling the stir he had caused at the DTF meeting earlier that morning, Norton couldn't resist smiling at Bendix.

She was quick to respond. "We're after bigger fish than Garrett, Commissioner. If we pick him up, we stop one shipment of drugs and lose the opportunity to nail the bastards who are behind this."

"That makes sense, Lieutenant," Kary nodded.

As they landed, Norton offered, "Fortunately for us, Garrett isn't quite as smart as he thinks he is. So, we'll continue to let that fish run 'til we're ready to reel him in."

Chapter 9

The intruder drove south on Route 16, passing a state welcome center, and continuing until he arrived at the northern border of North Conway. An historic downhill skiing center, North Conway was once a quaint village that offered beautiful, unimpeded views of Mt. Washington and the Presidentials. However, since the early 1980s, the village's character had been besieged by shopping outlets, restaurants, and commercial lodgings.

By the time the intruder arrived in North Conway late that morning, Route 16 was filled with automobiles and pedestrian traffic, as thousands of people were taking advantage of numerous shopping bargains and interesting dining opportunities situated along the road.

Under normal circumstances, the intruder tended to avoid eating breakfast or lunch when he was on a job. However, something about having murdered the old man earlier that morning was making him hungry. Despite strict orders to head directly toward his rendezvous, the intruder decided to stop when he spotted a colorful sign bearing the image of a large peach. He pulled over to the west side of Route 16 and parked his car. The single story, beautifully landscaped Peaches Restaurant lured him off the road. In this instance, it was a case of seeing a nice place to stop at precisely the wrong time.

Because the intruder was a party of one, the hostess was able to seat him at a glass-topped table for four immediately inside the doorway. The time on the wall clock was 11:20 a.m. If his waitress had any thoughts about engaging the intruder in pleasant conversation, she need not have bothered. The intruder ignored the menu, which contained items as diverse as quesadillas, omelets, and cinnamon bread French toast. Without making eye contact, the intruder requested a double order of scrambled eggs with wheat toast and black coffee. While he waited for his meal to arrive, he removed an iPhone from his pocket and called up Waze. The app indicated that his destination, the Green Granite Inn, was situated on the left side of Route 16, two miles south of where he was seated at that moment.

As he waited for his breakfast, the intruder sent a text message to the person he was meeting to say he would be there in fifteen minutes. The brief return message read, "#10, 2 knocks."

When the waitress brought his food, she was not at all surprised to be greeted in a monotone. "Just leave the food and my check."

As she passed her girlfriend who was waiting on a nearby table, the waitress said softly, "This one's a real charmer. I'll bet he stiffs me on the tip." However, now in a hurry, the intruder left her a twenty dollar bill for a breakfast that cost seven, including the nine percent meals tax.

Chapter 10

Standing next to his Malibu outside of the Peaches Restaurant, the intruder looked around to see if he was being followed. Seeing no one suspicious, he unlocked the car, entered, started the engine and pulled out into traffic, heading south on Route 16.

Before several minutes passed, he spotted the sign for the Green Granite Inn. From a distance, the sign itself looked to the intruder like a large green tombstone. On closer inspection, there was an image of a massive north country moose wading in a pond, with the name of the inn displayed prominently in large gold letters.

The lodging itself had an inviting appearance. The main building was

Dutch Colonial, with a cupola on the roof and a large portico providing shelter for the lobby entrance. The property was a large, two-story motel, not an inn as the sign advertised. The intruder's bosses had chosen this rendezvous site carefully. Had the two men from the cartel actually been staying overnight in an inn, it would have required the cartel members to enter an inside hallway through a large lobby. Thus, the likelihood of them being identified would have been greater. However, because the Green Granite was really a motel, the intruder was able to pull his car into a parking place in front of room ten, and enter directly from the parking lot.

※ ※ ※ ※ ※ ※

At 10:40, as Kary, Bendix and Norton exited the helicopter, they were greeted by two officers from the New Hampshire Major Crimes Unit, one a lieutenant and the other a sergeant. No introductions were necessary for Bendix and Norton, as they all had worked together in the field on previous occasions. Bendix quickly introduced Kary to Lieutenant Hollister and Trooper Robison.

Hollister spoke first to Kary. "It's nice to meet you, Commissioner. Of course, we knew that the governor had created a division to look after crimes against visitors' persons and property. I just hope this terrible murder doesn't prove to be too much for you... this being your first opportunity to get your feet wet." As Hollister said this, he winked at the three other officers.

This might have put Kary in an uncomfortable position, given the important role that state troopers played during investigations, were it not for the intervention of both Bendix and Norton.

Norton was defensive to the point of being aggressive.

"With all due respect, Lieutenant, maybe you didn't catch the commissioner's full name. This man isn't some greenhorn, political appointment. Dr. Turnell here has quite a reputation as a criminologist."

Bendix saw a need to quickly cool the situation. "What

my colleague is trying to say in his usual tactless way, Lieutenant, is that the commissioner is one of us. He's been walking the walk for years."

Sensing that the lieutenant had placed everyone in an uncomfortable position, Kary quickly dealt with the situation.

Removing his hat from his head, he smiled at the three officers. "It must be this fedora. This hat has gotten me in more hot water than you can possibly imagine." Putting it back on his head, he continued, "Please give my fedora some time. You all may actually grow to appreciate it."

Kary quietly thanked Bendix and Norton for their support, then asked Hollister and Robison to bring his team up to speed on the case.

"For starters, a gentleman named Arnold Dean died under questionable circumstances in the base station men's room this morning."

"Has anyone reached a conclusion about the cause of death?" Kary replied.

"According to the county coroner, his wind pipe was crushed by what appears to have been at least two hard punches."

"Kary replied, "We learned in transit that your coroner is estimating time of death at approximately 0755. Is that still the case?"

Robison replied, "We think he died just about that time."

"What's your basis for that conclusion?" Kary asked.

"We interviewed the director of marketing," then looking at his field notebook, he added, "a Ms. Bella Michaels."

"What did this Ms. Michaels tell you?" Bendix asked.

"She said that Mr. Dean had purchased a ticket online for the steam train," Robison replied. "She said he was a lifelong fan of steam trains, and today's ride was at the top of his bucket list."

"An unfortunate turn of phrase," Kary said with a wry smile. "Am I correct that there is only one steam train each day?" he asked.

"You're correct, Commissioner. The Cog's owners began mainly using diesel engines in 2008, but the first coach each morning is still pushed up the mountain by steam."

"Then, we're sure that Mr. Dean was here in time to catch that first train at 8:00 a.m.?" Kary questioned.

"It would appear so. We've asked Ms. Michaels to show us the footage from this morning's CCTV coverage."

"Excellent. Please keep going with your update," Kary said. As he talked, he began to walk up the hill toward the Base Station, with the others following him.

Hollister and Robison told Kary and the others that no ticket was found on Dean's body.

"I think we can safely presume that the person who did this isn't a steam train aficionado," Kary said.

"So, you think his motivation was…?" Norton began to ask.

"…Time, Sergeant. Time was the motivating factor here," Kary replied.

Kary's quick stride soon took him several yards ahead of the others. Now, walking backward without breaking stride, he said, "Please continue your appraisal, gentlemen."

Watching this seventy year old in action, with his fedora, his rapid stride and even quicker mind, Hollister looked at the other officers and flashed them a surreptitious thumbs up. Hollister had never met Kary before, but ten minutes with the man told the lieutenant that he was the real deal.

As the four came closer to the base station, Kary addressed the others.

"It's apparent that this perp needed to be on that first train, which would suggest that he was on a schedule that could not be broken."

"It makes sense that he was going to meet someone at the summit," Bendix agreed. "But, why the rush? There was a diesel-powered coach leaving within a short time."

"Maybe he didn't know that," Norton offered. For which he received a nod and a thumbs up from Kary.

"I'm told you already have a solid lead on who this murderer was going to meet," Kary said to the other two officers.

"You must be referring to Ned Garrett," Robison replied. "We know that he purchased a ticket on the Stage early this morning." It was a reference to the tour van that travels up the auto road.

"And we're certain that Garrett took a ride to the summit?" Kary asked.

Robison nodded. "We've had a tail on Garrett since last night. We know he crossed the Canadian border right after midnight. He was spotted entering the Stage building where he purchased a ticket to the summit."

"Garrett was aboard the first stage out this morning. Unfortunately, a small group of people showed up for tickets before our man could buy one. The van was full, or we'd have had someone traveling to the summit with him.

"We're getting somewhere," Kary replied. "Now, all we need to do is find a means for linking the two men."

"I may be able to help with that," another voice came from the doorway of the base station.

Kary turned around and was face to face with a small brunette woman in her late thirties. Her broad smile belied what had clearly been a stressful morning for the entire staff at the base station.

"You must be Ms. Michaels," he said as the two shook hands.

"That's amazing! How did you know my name?" she asked excitedly.

"There's nothing amazing at all, young lady. I've heard from these officers what a big help you've already been this morning." Then as he leaned toward Michaels, Kary said in a voice only she could hear, "Beside that, I'm reading your name tag."

The young marketing director possessed information that would prove helpful for the investigative team. However, before she could provide it, Robison had an update.

Robison told the investigators, "We've been tracking Garrett ever since Lieutenant Hollister ordered me to let him leave the premises."

"That was a good decision, one that Director Williams and I made jointly," Kary informed him.

"Where is he right now?" Hollister asked Robison.

"He left here at 1050. We've been tailing his Malibu using a series of unmarked cars," Robison reported.

"I'm impressed you were able to handle the logistics for that so quickly," Kary told Hollister.

"It was a matter of necessity being the mother of invention," Hollister replied. "We made a quick call to our Troop F headquarters in Twin Mountain. I told them we needed at least three to five unmarked cars on the road ASAP. The cars we're using belong to troopers, administrative assistants…one is even owned by the custodian."

Kary smiled at Hollister's ingenuity, placing his hand on the lieutenant's shoulder for emphasis. Next, turning to Robison, he asked him to continue his report.

"Garrett left here about ten minutes before you all landed. We know he pulled into Fabyan's station on Route 302. The state trooper tailing him said he was in the restaurant only long enough to grab a cup of coffee. He left and stopped next door for gas. Lieutenant Hollister ordered another of our officers to pursue him at a distance from there."

"What did he do next?" Kary asked.

"He turned right on Route 3 and has been driving north ever since."

Kary said to Robison, "It's almost 1100; so I think we can safely presume he's either headed for the crossing at Beecher Falls or the one at Pittsburg. Am I right?"

Robison replied, "I feel certain that he wants to get back across the border as soon as possible. If my suspicion is correct, Garrett's carrying something he doesn't want to be caught with."

"So, where do you think he'll cross the border, officer?"

"Beecher Falls is closer. He'll reach there at just about 1235, ninety-five minutes from now."

At that moment, Hollister asserted, "I think we need to stop Garrett before he crosses into Quebec."

But, Kary disagreed, speaking to the lieutenant in a calm voice, "Before you issue that directive, let's think about this a moment."

"What's to think about, Commissioner? Garrett is getting away with tens of thousands of dollars in drug money," Norton said.

"We have at least a half hour before anyone needs to be notified," Kary reminded them.

Bendix asked, "What are you thinking, Commissioner?"

"Let's review the situation. On the one hand, you have a known drug carrier who is headed to the international border with a bunch of money hidden somewhere in his car." Everyone nodded in agreement and Kary continued. "On the other hand, we have a DB in the base station. At present, it appears likely the killer is a confederate of Garrett's."

Several of the others protested. "But, we don't really know that... not yet."

"True," Kary agreed. "I'm willing to gamble that we'll have time to deal with Garrett. However, if he gets stopped, the cartel will be alerted that something has happened."

Norton argued, "Not if we can get to him before he can use his cell phone."

This time, it was Lieutenant Hollister who argued against his own idea.

"That's not necessarily true, sergeant. Garrett is an experienced mule. And, from what we've learned in our meetings, the people he is working for have proven themselves to be damned clever."

Norton shrugged.

Hollister continued. "No doubt they've worked out a regularly scheduled contact plan."

Kary added his support for what Hollister said. "The lieutenant is spot on. If we detain Garrett, other members of the cartel will be alerted when he fails to contact them. If that's the case, they'll disappear... including Dean's killer. That would be a disaster."

"Okay, Commissioner. It looks like we'll play this your way, even if it means losing Garrett and the money he's delivering," Hollister concurred.

Bendix had thought about the situation carefully. "Even if we allow him to cross the border, it doesn't mean we've lost him or his money."

Hollister asked Bendix to explain.

"Some of you may not be aware of this, including you, Commissioner," she continued, "WADA is located in Montreal."

"WADA?" Kary questioned her.

"Yes, it's the World Anti-Doping Agency, an organization that sets anti-juicing policies, rules and regulations internationally," she replied.

Norton asked Bendix, "I'm familiar with WADA, Lieutenant; but how does that help us?"

"Think of it this way, Sergeant. Canada and the U.S. are both members of WADA. So, there is the potential for cooperation in monitoring Garrett once he crosses the border."

"Then why haven't they done this before now?" Norton argued.

"Actually, we have been working with the Sûreté du Québec," she replied.

"What is the Sûreté…?" Kary started to ask.

"They're the equivalent of us," Hollister told him.

"The Sûreté has been keeping tabs on Garrett for several months," Bendix smiled. Then, as an aside to Kary, she added, "You'll know all about this stuff after you've been hanging around with DTF for a while."

Hollister issued a new order to Robison, "I want updates on Garrett's whereabouts every ten minutes, until 1215; then I want them delivered to us continuously. Is that clear, Trooper?"

"Yes, Lieutenant," Robison replied briskly.

※ ※ ※ ※ ※ ※

When Kary asked Norton to take Robison and go on an errand, the sergeant was displeased, and didn't make an effort to hide the fact. Kary told him the pair needed to confirm the information they'd received about Garrett's visit to Fabyan's restaurant.

"Why can't Robison do that by himself?"

Kary knew that any hope of a meaningful long-term working relationship with Norton could hinge on his response.

"Look, Sergeant. I know this may seem like a make-work errand to you. It's anything but that. We have the state trooper's visual that Garrett stopped at Fabyan's on his way back to Quebec City. However, we don't know what he did while he was inside."

Norton knew that he had little choice but to follow orders, but he wasn't done learning the reason behind them. Even though he'd developed instant respect for Kary, Norton couldn't suppress his nature to question authority. Also, Norton knew the commissioner was not going to be his boss in the long term.

Kary stood firm. "I need you to interview anyone who may have talked to Garrett and, while you're doing that, Robison needs to put on a pair of evidence scene gloves and sift through the trash barrels."

Norton whistled. "Great… he's going to love doing that," he replied.

"Actually, he probably won't. But, you won't have any

trouble issuing an order, will you, Sergeant?" When Norton looked at Kary with a quizzical expression on his face, Kary placed his hand firmly on the younger man's shoulder and said, "Trust me, it won't be a problem. For one thing, you outrank him, just like I outrank you. And, in your case, there's a matter of those black belts," he added with a smile.

Kary had no further problem with Norton after that conversation.

Bendix waited for Kary to finish talking with Norton.

"So, what's next, Commissioner?" she questioned.

Kary asked Bendix to bring Director Williams up-to-date via email, then to join Bella Michaels and him in the Cog's administrative offices as soon as she was finished.

Michaels met Kary at the base of a stairwell, just inside of the entrance to the building. She asked if there was specific information she could get for him. Kary replied that he needed to see a copy of Arnold Dean's electronic transaction and, if possible, a copy of his ticket. Once they reached Michael's office on the top floor of the base station, she punched a few numbers into her office telephone and spoke to the person on the other end of the line.

Hanging up the receiver, Michaels told Kary that she'd have that information for him in a matter of minutes. Next, she logged into her computer and went directly to her email page.

"Commissioner, I have some information that may prove helpful to you," Michaels informed him. "I have two emails from Mr. Dean that I'd like to show you. I must tell you that these are rather unusual."

Looking over her shoulder at the computer screen, Kary asked, "How are they unusual?"

"Well, first of all, prospective customers don't typically communicate with me. They use the online system to order tickets, and that's usually the end of that."

"But not with Mr. Dean?" Kary asked.

"No, not at all. He wanted me to know how excited he was to be taking the steam engine to the summit," Michaels replied. "He told me that this was something he was waiting to do for nearly fifty years. You could actually sense the joy he was feeling by reading his note." Michaels began to tear up as she said this. "One other thing;" she added, "he wanted to be certain that his space on the first coach was guaranteed. But, the way he stated things made him seem like a very sweet man."

"As I understand it, the first coach is the only one each day that's powered by your steam engine." He paused, "Did he ever contact you again?"

"Yes. That was the unusual part. Almost always, when people order a ticket online, they want to receive it via email, then print it off at home," she replied.

"Why didn't Dean want to do things that way?" Kary asked.

"I suspect there may have been two reasons. Either he didn't have a printer attached to his computer," she began.

"Or… ?"

"Or else, he wanted it printed on ticket stock. That way,

his ticket would look like the ones we print on the premises… a kind of collector's item."

As they waited for Lieutenant Bendix to arrive, there was a knock on the office door. It was a member of the ticketing department's staff with copies of Dean's ticket and a paper copy of his online transaction. Kary perused these materials. They showed that Dean had purchased his ticket using a Visa credit card. The ticket clearly identified the time of departure and had the ticket holder's name printed on it.

Two minutes later, there was a second knock on the door. Lieutenant Bendix had finished communicating with Director Williams, then climbed the flight of stairs to Michael's office. Once Bendix was in the room, Kary asked the marketing director to call up the footage from the CCTV camera that focused on the passenger loading platform. After several minutes of searching, Michaels found the portion that showed the time to be 0745. As she was about to start the footage, a thought occurred to Kary.

Turning to Bendix, he asked, "Lieutenant, will you please contact Sergeant Norton and tell him to come up here with Trooper Robison as soon as they get back on site."

By coincidence, Bendix's cell phone rang a few seconds later. It was Norton on the phone. Sitting several feet away, Kary could hear the excitement in the sergeant's voice. Bendix listened for thirty seconds, told Norton that he was needed back at the base station ASAP, then handed Kary her cell phone. As she did this, Bendix told Kary, "Norton says he owes you an apology. What's that about?"

Kary smiled and shrugged at Bendix as he placed the phone next to his ear. When he had disconnected the call, he turned to Bendix, whose curiosity was in overdrive.

"I sent the sergeant and Robison down to Fabyan's to search for evidence about Garrett," he told her.

"I overheard, and Norton clearly wasn't excited about the assignment," she replied.

"That's an understatement," Kary replied. "But, the two of them did as I asked. Norton didn't turn up much from his interviews with the manager, but the busboy remembered that Garrett ordered a burger and a black coffee to go, then went to the men's room before hitting the road. That's where Robison struck the motherlode. Robison did a bit of trash diving in the men's room. I had hunch we might find something useful, but what they found exceeded my expectations."

"What did they find?" Bendix was having trouble maintaining her characteristic nonchalant veneer.

"It appears they found Arnold Dean's ticket from this morning," he smiled.

Chapter 11

At 11:55, the intruder parked his car directly in front of room ten at the Green Granite Inn. Per instructions, he knocked twice on the door and waited. A minute passed before he heard the unmistakable clicking sound of a revolver being cocked. Next, the peep hole on the door darkened.

The intruder said sarcastically, "You people don't take chances, do you?"

"A deep voice came from behind the door. "Take a step back and hold your arms out to your sides. Keep the backpack out where I can see it."

The man behind the door was satisfied but still did not allow the intruder inside the room.

"Is anyone out there with you?" he asked the intruder. "Were you followed?"

Informed that the answer to both questions was negative, the man behind the door continued, "Here's how this is going to play out. When I tell you, you're going to open the door, step inside, then shut the door behind you."

"I suppose I can do all that," came the intruder's attempt at cynicism.

"Listen to me, asshole. I don't want to hear your voice, not unless I ask you to talk. Otherwise, keep your stinking trap shut." When the intruder said nothing, the voice demanded, "Do you understand what I'm saying?"

The intruder was losing patience fast. Standing there, he mulled over the idea of turning over the stuff to this idiot, then coming back with his Glock. "I'd love to show this guy who the asshole is," he told himself.

But, instead, he replied, "Yeah, I understand."

"That's a good boy," the voice from behind the door told him. "So, here's the rest of what you're going to do. Once you've shut the door, you'll toss your backpack onto the second bed from the door. Are you following me so far?"

The intruder sighed. "Yeah, I understand."

"Good. Then the next thing you're going to do is remove all of your clothes, stand there with your legs apart, bent over toward the front of the room."

"You're shitting me, right?" the intruder growled.

"No. I'm not shitting you. This is your first time working for us. We need to make sure your delivery is complete," he replied. "The stuff you're carrying is valuable. We can't tolerate anyone stealing from us."

"I haven't stolen anything from you, mister. Frankly, it pisses me off that you're treating me like this," the intruder told him.

"Yeah, sure. You're such a good person; you would never do anything dishonest…like hell you wouldn't. We vetted you; we know all about your past dealings. So, here's your choice. You can leave the stuff outside by the door and forget about being paid, or you can do what I just told you."

The intruder considered turning around and driving away with the backpack.

As if the man behind the door was reading his mind, the voice continued.

"Don't even think about making a runner. One more thing; leave your car key on the chair outside the room. We'll do a thorough search of the Malibu while you're inside.

Had the late Arnold Dean been there, he would have appreciated the irony of the intruder standing buck naked and bent over... his personal space being violated by someone he didn't even know.

Chapter 12

Once Norton and Robison arrived in Bella Michaels' office, Kary stood up and congratulated them for a job well done.

Norton confessed to Kary that he thought the commissioner had sent the pair on a fool's errand. Norton admitted that Kary was one commissioner who actually understood how field investigations work.

"That's because he wrote the book on this stuff, you dummy," Bendix couldn't resist chiding Norton.

Kary called Robison over to the screen, where Michaels had paused that morning's CCTV footage at 0750.

"Trooper Robison, I want you to take a look at this video and tell me what you see," Kary told him.

Robison watched a sixty second clip, then asked to watch it one more time. After they watched the clip a second time, Robison asked Michaels if she could zoom in on two people on the screen.

"Robison pointed at an elderly man and exclaimed, "That looks like our vic."

Norton asked Michaels to zoom out one more time. "What's he doing right now?" the sergeant asked.

"It appears he just removed a ticket from an inside pocket in his parka," Bendix replied.

"And he's so happy that he's kissing it," Michaels added

while feeling her emotions rising again. "That poor lovely man; he never got his ride to the summit."

Kary asked Michaels to zoom in on a second man; this one was wearing a light color parka and a dark baseball cap, and carrying a backpack that appeared to be a similar shade as his parka. He was clearly several decades younger than Arnold Dean.

"Look how closely this guy is watching Mr. Dean," Kary told the others. "I just wish this was in color, not black and white."

Michaels apologized to the others. "For our normal purposes, color is an unnecessary expense," she added.

Everyone's attention returned to the footage on the screen. "Look how the guy with the backpack doesn't take his eyes off our vic," Bendix agreed. "Let's zoom back out and see what happens."

The image showed Dean looking at his watch, turning and heading back inside the base station.

"The poor guy must have made the decision that he couldn't wait until reaching the summit to go to the bathroom," Bendix told them.

"Look at that," Norton pointed at the screen. "The guy who was watching Dean is following him back inside the building. He's not even trying to be subtle."

"This tells us a lot," Kary said.

"I agree," Bendix added. "The other man seems to have the means, the motive and the opportunity."

Michaels was overhearing all of this. "May I ask what

all of that means?" she asked.

"It's crime investigation talk," Norton told her in a tone that was a little too

patronizing for Bendix's taste. She shot Norton a disapproving look. Realizing his mistake, Norton adjusted his tone. "Motive refers to the presence of an apparent reason for committing a crime."

"In this instance, the perpetrator must have had a reason to steal a ticket, to be on the first train out of the station," Kary told her.

Michaels nodded to show that she understood. "That train was sold out," she reminded them.

At that moment, a thought occurred to Kary. "I wonder if anyone at the ticket booth recalls having been asked to sell a ticket at the last minute."

"I'll find out right away," Michaels said excitedly.

"No doubt he would have been rather anxious," Bendix told her.

"Should I mention anything about the way he was dressed?" Michaels asked.

"No, please don't do that. I don't want people creating false memories to satisfy our needs. Witnesses have a tendency to do that," Kary added.

Norton began explaining the term 'means' to the marketing manager.

"Means is our way of saying that he had the capability of carrying out the act, be it an assault on a person or property," he added.

"I'm afraid that the opportunity is obvious," Kary told her. "Apparently, Mr. Dean was in your small men's room. The perpetrator no doubt waited outside until he was certain he could be alone with Dean. The clock was ticking, and he really wanted that ticket."

Bendix took up the description of what may have happened.

"One of two things happened next," she began. "Either Dean dropped his ticket on the floor and the perpetrator picked it up, or the perpetrator came into the stall and took it."

"I'd say it was option A," Kary told the others. "Dean would have locked the stall door before sitting on the toilet. And, I seriously doubt he would have risked opening it for a stranger. Besides that, the noise would have attracted attention. My guess is he dropped his ticket on the floor and the perp started to leave with it. When Dean opened the door to confront the perpetrator, that was his last act."

Ever the skeptic, Norton said, "Of course, it could have been option B."

Kary smiled at Norton. He appreciated the young sergeant's moxie.

"That's true, Sergeant. And you know how we'll determine which one of us is correct, don't you?"

Norton thought for a minute before replying, "Yeah. Forensics and the autopsy will show whether Dean had finished his business or not."

"That is so gross!" Michaels exclaimed.

During the short discussion about means, motive and opportunity, Kary had not yet asked Robison what he needed to know.

"Trooper Robison, you've had an opportunity to see Garrett up close and our suspected perpetrator on the CCTV footage. Is this the man you talked with in the parking lot earlier?"

"No, Commissioner. That's definitely not him."

"How can you be so sure about that, Robison," Norton asked.

"It's pretty simple, really. Garrett and this guy were dressed almost exactly alike. When I first saw him, Garrett was still wearing a gray parka with a matching backpack. He had on a navy blue ball cap with 'Cog Railway' written on it."

"This guy does, too," Norton chided.

"I know, Sergeant. But, I'm telling you, the two don't look the same." Robison asked Michaels to provide a close up of the suspected perpetrator's face. While the image wasn't crystal clear, the man's facial features could be distinguished. Pointing to the computer screen, Robison told the others, "Garrett has an oval face with a square jaw. His eyes are dark, probably brown. This guy has a freakishly pointed chin, and look at his eyes… they're really light… almost haunting," he added.

A soft knock on the door produced a visit from the same staff member who had been there earlier. Because the phone lines in the ticket office were all busy, she produced a single sheet of handwritten information for Michaels, then headed back downstairs.

Michaels showed Kary and the others the note. There had been no emails requesting a ticket at the last minute. However, one member of the ticket office recalled an insistent conversation early that morning, probably at around 7:30. She said that a man offered her a hundred dollar bill if she could find him a space in the first coach of the day. When the ticket person said she could find a seat on the second train, the man had looked at her menacingly, before stalking off. The ticket person concluded, "I'll never forget the look in those scary gray eyes of his."

Michaels reminded the others, "As I told you earlier, our steam trains are very popular. With the weather forecasters saying that the atmosphere would be the clearest it's been all month, every ticket was gone more than a week ago."

While the others were discussing the intruder, Robison's cell phone rang. He stepped out into the second floor hallway to take the call, which was from one of the state troopers following Garrett. Robison listened, thanked the trooper, then ended the connection. He immediately called Lieutenant Hollister to share this update.

While Kary, Bendix, Norton and Robison were meeting with the marketing director on the second floor, Hollister was busy supervising activities at the crime scene on the main floor of the base station. The lieutenant had several responsibilities, including overseeing the forensics team and interviewing any witnesses. While being cooped up in a small men's room with the smell of death in his nostrils may have dampened a lesser man's resolve, Hollister had good reason to be in a positive frame of mind. Important evidence was being found.

Setting his phone on speaker, Robison reported what he had just learned from the state trooper in the field.

Hollister spoke into his cell phone. "Are you there, Commissioner?" When Kary said he was listening, Hollister continued, "We've just had two important developments, one which requires immediate attention. Despite the fact that Robison had received the call from the field, protocol dictated that the lieutenant share the information with his superiors, this included Kary.

"What do you have, Lieutenant?" Kary asked.

"Robison just received an update on Garrett's whereabouts," Hollister replied.

"What's the news, Lieutenant?" Kary asked.

"He's just entering Lancaster," Hollister replied. "That's a little more than one hour from the Beecher Falls border crossing. How do you want to proceed, Commissioner?"

Kary replied, "Keep an eye on him," Kary replied. "But, I'm still prepared to let him enter Canada, if necessary."

"Do you want us to do a search of his vehicle?" Hollister asked.

"Not at this time. What I do want is the VIN from his car. Please alert the border patrol that we may want them to detain Garrett as soon as he arrives. It's also possible that we'll want to have your counterparts in Quebec detain Garrett."

"Understood. I'll take care of this right away," Hollister replied. However, he wasn't prepared to end the conversation, as there was more information to share.

Hollister asked Kary if Bendix was listening to their conversation. When she told the lieutenant that she could hear what was being said, the lieutenant continued.

"Forensics has lifted two prints from the lenses of the vic's glasses. We've done a quick visual of Dean's fingers, and one set appears to be his; the bifurcations and whorls appear to match. The second set is not Dean's."

Kary watched Bendix's expression brighten considerably when she heard this. She appeared to be licking her lips at the prospect of leading a fingerprint scan.

"I presume you obtained those using superglue fuming," she said. "Without waiting for Hollister's response, she continued, "Please have someone forward those to me right away. As you know, we'll need to send the image of the lifted print and the original to the state crime lab in Concord."

"Let's not forget about the partial facial image we have of the perp standing on the passenger platform," Norton reminded them.

Bendix added, "It is a fairly clear image, especially given the fact that it was taken from at least ten yards away. And Norton's right, we should send both items to Concord right away. So, if you'll forward the fingerprint to me, we'll have someone in the lab at headquarters give us a preliminary ID."

Hollister appeared dubious. "Those folks are pretty backed up. I just hope you can find a way around their log-jam," he replied.

At this point, Kary interjected, "Let me worry about that, Lieutenant. I have the governor on speed dial as we speak. We'll get this information back pronto, or he can find himself another commissioner."

As Hollister was about to return to the men's room, one of his officers approached him.

"Lieutenant, these are the Johnsons from Waltham, Mass. I think you're going to want to hear what Mrs. Johnson has to say."

Mrs. Johnson's information proved to be a game changer.

※ ※ ※ ※ ※ ※

Once Kary returned Robison's cell phone to him, he turned to Michaels and asked her, "Is there CCTV coverage on the summit?"

"Yes, there is," she replied. "Unfortunately, it's pretty much limited to the entry way of the Adams Building."

"Is there any way to look at it down here?" he asked.

Michaels shook her head, no.

"Then, if the mountain won't come to Mohammed..." he began.

Michaels made a call to the people staffing the State Park desk at the summit. Within minutes she had arranged for the footage to be loaded and available for viewing on a computer at the summit.

When she asked Kary whether he and his team wanted to ride up to the top of the mountain on the Cog, he replied, "I'm afraid we'll need to take a rain check on your offer, as time is of the essence. Beside that, Sergeant Norton tells me there's a nice helicopter pad on top and the wind is only blowing at twenty knots. So, we will be saying goodbye and thank you for all of your assistance."

"I'm more than happy to help," she replied. "I never met Mr. Dean face-to-face, but from everything I've learned about him, he must have been a very nice man."

"He certainly didn't deserve to be killed... not even for a Cog railway ticket," Kary said with a wry smile.

They could not have picked a more perfect day for the helicopter trip to the summit. The air was crystal clear as they followed the route of the Cog railway. Despite the urgency of the situation, Kary marveled at the juxtaposition of green vegetation, blue skies, and the variety of gray and pink hues given off by the rocks below. He watched as the vegetation changed from beautiful broadleaf trees at the base station, to dark evergreens, until there was a tundra-like landscape of bare rock and ground hugging scrub vegetation near the summit. Also, the engineering feat that produced the trestle at Jacob's Ladder did not escape his perceptive eyes.

It was 12:10 when the pilot landed on a paved space just below the summit. As the three members of Kary's team walked from the helicopter, each commented on how far in the distance there was visibility.

"We must be able to see more than a hundred miles," Norton marveled. "Look," he said while pointing to the east, "That's the Atlantic Ocean;" then turning around, he pointed, "Those must be the Green Mountains over there."

This caused Kary to jest, "If we had a powerful enough telescope, we could watch Garrett's Malibu being detained at the Canadian border."

This caused Bendix and Norton to smile and shake their heads.

The three made their way to the Sherman Adams building. As they entered, Bendix pointed above the main entryway to the place where a CCTV camera was mounted.

"That should give us the footage we need...I hope," Kary told Norton and her.

When they entered the building, Norton, who had visited a year earlier, led the way through a veritable mob of sightseers. He located the State Park desk staffed by two men and a woman. One of the men recognized Norton and quickly escorted the team into a small office where the CCTV footage was already loaded.

Bendix sat down at the computer. Soon, the desired time, 0900, appeared on the screen.

"Let's see what we can find out," Kary said.

The time on the screen read 0905 when the image of Garrett first appeared in the footage.

"That's Garrett," Norton pointed at the remarkably clear picture on the screen. Garrett stood in the doorway for about a minute, then disappeared off the right side of the screen, probably to enter the Adams building. He was absent for approximately five minutes before he reappeared and stood next to the entrance to the building.

Approximately ten minutes passed before a second male figure, attired similarly to the way Garrett was dressed, entered the building and passed right next to Garrett. There was no obvious indication that either man recognized the other. The other man, who they believed had arrived on the Cog railway after murdering Arnold Dean, remained inside the building for ten minutes.

"What the hell could he be doing all of this time?" Norton asked impatiently.

"Stay calm, Norton," Bendix told him. "I'm sure this is all part of a plan to divert suspicion from the two of them."

Kary agreed. "If they simply met, then walked out of the building together, it would make things too easy for us.

Those words had no sooner left Kary's lips when the image of the second man returned to screen. He passed by Garrett and kept walking through the doorway until his image disappeared from view. Less than a minute later, Garrett headed in the same direction.

The three watched the tape for several more minutes before Kary looked at Bendix and Norton.

"What are your thoughts?"

Norton spoke first. "It's obvious that there were two of them up here. For sure, we aren't just looking for Garrett."

Bendix agreed. "While we can't see exactly what colors

the two were wearing, it is apparent that the two men were dressed alike for a reason.

Kary told the pair, "I'd say those assessments are spot on; however, there are two questions that we need to answer."

"What questions, Commissioner?" Norton asked.

"First, why were they dressed alike?" Kary offered.

Bendix didn't wait for Kary to supply the second question. "Yes, and where did they go from here?"

Kary agreed. "It seems to me that the two men didn't know one another. The cartel must have instructed them to look for someone dressed the same."

"Also, the two of them were dressed alike and drove identical cars so they could easily switch places," Bendix marveled at the shrewdness of the cartel's plan.

"I think we'll need to do a bit of educated guessing to figure out where the two were headed when they left this building," Kary offered. "However, we can deduce that they pulled some kind of clever weave pattern, using this mountain as their setting. The plot is brilliant in its deviousness. From what you've told me, Garrett is an experienced drug mule. It's probable that he brought drugs from Quebec using some kind of hidden compartment in his car. For this exchange, he's been instructed to wear a navy baseball cap with his gray parka and backpack."

Norton, as usual, remained skeptical. "What does he hope to gain?"

"An easy escape," Bendix responded.

Norton suddenly began to catch on. "Yeah, I get it, He travels down the mountain on the opposite side, gets into another white Chevy Malibu, and heads back to Canada with his backpack full of American bucks."

"That's right, Sergeant. And their plan would have worked. No one from state law enforcement would have been any the wiser if the guy at the base station hadn't lost his cool and murdered a tourist."

"So, the guy who murdered Mr. Dean rode the Cog railway up the mountain then took the Stage van down to Glen," Bendix said.

"That's right," Kary replied. "Once he and Garrett met up here on the summit, Garrett relinquished the role of drug mule. Garrett came here transporting drugs, but left carrying money."

"So our murderer took the drugs into his possession and headed south down Route 16 where, no doubt, he'll meet someone from the cartel... but who is he meeting and where?" Norton said.

"That's the question we need to answer... and soon," Kary replied. "I recommend we start by seeing if we can figure out how they made the switch. It's information we need if we catch them."

"When we catch them," Norton corrected him.

They left the Adams Building hoping to trace the steps of the two drug mules. As they did, Kary's cell phone buzzed.

Kary looked at the screen on his phone. It was Lieutenant Hollister calling. He instructed Bendix and Norton to fan out to see if they could identify a likely place where the two cartel men may have exchanged drugs for money.

"How's it going up there, Kary?" Hollister asked.

"We've just looked at the CCTV footage," Kary told him. "We now know one thing for certain… not that there was much doubt. The tape showed two men dressed nearly alike."

Before dismissing the idea that Garrett could be working alone, Hollister asked, "Were they ever on the tape at the same time?"

"Yes, briefly, but long enough to be certain," Kary replied.

"That's great news," Hollister told him. "The tape corroborates evidence we just learned a few minutes ago."

"What evidence is that, Lieutenant?"

Hollister proceeded to tell Kary about a young couple named Johnson who had approached him while they were waiting for one of the diesel locomotives to take them up the mountain. He told Kary how this was going to be their second trip of the day.

"Riding the cog must be a fantastic experience," Kary replied. "But, why would someone ride up here and back, then turn around and do the same thing again in one day?"

Hollister told Kary he initially thought the Johnsons could be sketchy.

"It turns out the Johnsons work for Outside Magazine. They're doing a piece comparing the experience of riding up the cog using the old steam engine versus modern diesel technology."

"So, what does this have to do with our investigation?" Kary asked.

"Apparently, they sat next to our alleged murderer on the way up the mountain. They said he was the last one to board the coach and barely made it on time. He sat next to Ms. Johnson and never spoke a word directly to them until they were almost at the summit. The guy made it apparent that he didn't want to make conversation. When the coach arrived at the summit, he disappeared."

"Was that the last they saw of him?" Kary asked.

"Yes… and, no," Hollister replied.

"Yes and no. What the heck does that mean, Lieutenant?"

"I'll explain. When it came time to board the coach for the trip back down the mountain, they saw that the guy in the gray parka was already inside. The couple took the seat across the aisle from the man. Only thing, it wasn't the same guy. Mrs. Johnson spotted a distinct difference right away."

"What did she see?" Kary asked.

"The guy's eyes. She had been mesmerized by the gray eyes of the fellow sitting next to her on the way up. When she snuck another look at the guy on the way down, the new guy's eyes were as dark as coffee beans."

"This is just the kind of information we need, Lieutenant. We have about fifteen minutes of work to do up here before we head to the helicopter. Let's touch bases once we're airborne."

Kary closed the connection on his iPhone and started walking up a gravel path. Ahead of him, he saw Bendix and Norton leaning against a rock wall just below the Tip Top House.

The Tip Top House was a one and one-half story former hotel that was built in 1853, more than a decade before the Cog Railway opened for business. It's rough granite walls had been mortared together to provide the necessary strength to fend off the infamous winds on the mountain. The building was situated on the southwest side of the summit, mere yards away from both the cog station and the parking lot at the end of the auto road.

It was the Tip Top House's proximal location to both forms of transportation that convinced Bendix and Norton that the former hotel was probably where the two mules had exchanged their cargoes.

The three investigators entered the building and walked all the way to the back of the main room.

"This wouldn't have worked. It's too public," Norton told Kary and Bendix. The sergeant had some familiarity with the inside of the building. So, he felt fairly certain that he knew where the exchange had transpired. Norton led Kary and Bendix into a parallel room, which served as a bunkroom, containing bed frames designed to hold nine total bedrolls.

"What do you think, Commissioner?"

"I'm not sure, Sergeant. This room has less public traffic than the main one. But, what if they were interrupted while handing off the goods?" Kary asked.

Norton thought for a minute before an idea occurred to him. "What if they didn't hand off the goods… suppose they just swapped the backpacks," he declared.

Bendix was dubious at first. "I don't know, Norton. Two men walking around in this small building wearing identical outfits. I'm not convinced."

However, Kary was persuaded, but suggested a small variation to the plan.

"We saw that the two men left the Adams building separately. What if one of them came in here first, removed his backpack, and left it on a predetermined bunk, then closed the curtain and walked back into the main room."

This idea intrigued Bendix. "I get it now. So, then the second guy walks in, removes his backpack and puts it in the same bed, while taking the first guy's stuff with him."

Norton continued the discussion. "Right… so then the first guy walks back into the room and picks up the other backpack. I'm guessing that neither one of them went back into the Adams building. They must have switched their tickets and car keys by leaving them inside the backpacks."

"I'll have to admit, as much as it pains me to say this, whoever orchestrated all of this is one clever person," Bendix said.

"The commissioner's right, Lieutenant. We'd never have caught onto their plan if Arnold Dean wasn't murdered in the base station," Norton said.

Bendix added, "And, I'd guess neither Garrett nor the person awaiting the drugs at the other end has any idea that the second mule committed cold-blooded murder."

Kary looked at his two associates. "And that's precisely how we're going to catch them."

Chapter 13

As Robison had projected, it was 1235 when Garrett arrived at the border ...twenty-five minutes before Kary and the others lifted off from the summit of Mt. Washington.

If Garrett thought he was going to pass through Canadian customs with a mere tip of the hat, he was mistaken. When the officer in charge of the Beecher Falls border crossing heard from Bill Williams, director of the NHDTF, he was more than happy to assist. While Williams made it clear that the Canadians should not detain Garrett officially, he requested that steps be taken to delay the drug mule as long as feasible. A cleverly designed set of measures that had been used successfully in the past was immediately implemented by the Canadians.

As Garrett pulled up to the border, he was directed toward one of three booths, the farthest from the entry point. Next, the border guard who was assigned to interview Garrett pretended to speak only French. When it immediately became apparent that Garrett's command of the language was minimal, the border guard continued to ramble in French. Similar to the majority of U.S. citizens, Garrett had never taken the time to learn the primary language of Quebec province, despite the fact that he made his permanent residence there.

Sitting in his Malibu at the remarkably quiet border crossing, Garrett grew more and more frustrated with the situation he found himself in. However, he knew it would be foolish to cause a scene that could result in his car being searched by the border patrol. At that moment, Garrett remembered the one French phrase that he learned as a high school student, to be used in case of emergency.

"WC?" he asked the guard.

"Oui, oui, monsieur," came the reply. Then the guard pointed to a nearby men's room with a bright yellow sign on the door that read, "Ferme/Closed." Next, he pointed at a building situated one hundred yards away and said, "WC."

Garrett left his car at the booth and walked across a parking lot toward the men's room. When the drug mule was out of view, the border guard immediately removed a cell phone from his uniform jacket and took a picture of the VIN plate situated beneath the windshield wiper on the driver's side of the car. Within seconds, the VIN from Garrett's car was on its way to Bendix.

When Garrett returned from the men's room, he was relieved to see a new border guard standing in the booth where the francophone officer had been.

"Man, can you please process me through here, so I can head home?" Garrett asked.

"I'm afraid there's going to be a delay, sir," the English-speaking guard informed him.

"But, why?" Garrett cried as he removed a passport

from his pocket. "Can't you just look at this and let me through?"

The guard looked sorrowfully at Garrett. "No, sir. I can't. Our computers are frozen"

Garrett watched as two cars that had arrived just ahead of him were crossing the border. "Hey, what about those guys? They got through," he asked excitedly.

"What is it you people from the U.S. say… timing is everything," the guard replied. "The computer went down just as we finished processing them … and you were in the men's room. I apologize for this, sir. It hasn't happened in months. It's just bad luck for you. Hopefully, the delay won't be for much longer. Last time it took several hours to start working."

The guard was doing his best not to laugh at the ruse. "Here's what I recommend, sir. Pull your car over to the side and take a nap."

Of course, the guard knew very well the drug mule wasn't going to take a nap. Once he pulled his Malibu off to the side, Garrett used his phone to notify the cartel that he was temporarily delayed at the border. When cross-examined by his contact, he assured his employers that it was because of a computer glitch which would be resolved soon.

The two border guards watched as the light from Garrett's cell phone went dark and the car seat was leaned back in the sleep position. Unbeknownst to Garrett, one mile back down the road, New Hampshire and Vermont state police were rerouting traffic to the Norton, Vermont border station, so as to avoid arousing the drug mule's suspicion.

"It looks like he bought our little charade," one said to the other. To which the first guard replied with a large grin, "Oui." As they parted company, the pair enjoyed a hearty laugh.

Chapter 14

Aboard the helicopter, Bendix received the VIN from the car Garrett was driving. A quick comparison was made with the VIN from the car Garrett had left in the Stage parking lot that morning.

"Just as we thought," Bendix told Kary and Norton.

"What's up, Lieutenant?" Norton asked.

"We just received a photographic image of the VIN in the car Garrett has at the border," she replied. "As we suspected, the car he's driving may look like the one he drove down from Quebec, but it isn't the same car. There's one commonality: both VINs have seventeen numbers," she laughed.

Bendix continued, "However, we learned from our Quebec counterparts that the car Garrett was driving when he left Quebec City has a VIN that begins with 1J3MM. The one he's driving now has 2M4NN."

"That's perfect," Kary replied. This is just another piece of irrefutable evidence that there were two drug mules operating in tandem. I'll tell you this, once we catch the other guy, that murdering SOB, no hot-shot lawyer is going to get the charges dismissed due to insufficient evidence."

Bendix and Norton showed their approval by flashing thumbs up. Next,

Kary informed them that the team should head to North Conway and await news from Williams. He asked Bendix to find a suitable place where they could be picked up by a state police vehicle. She looked at her computer screen and reported that there were three options: the Apte Heliport, the Forbes Heliport, and the Memorial Hospital Heliport. When Kary asked Bendix which of the three had the easiest access to Route 16, she told him that the hospital site could have them on Route 16 in a matter of minutes.

※ ※ ※ ※ ※ ※

South of their position, in the Green Granite Inn, the relationship of the two cartel men had not improved. The intruder had hoped he could leave once the other guy from the cartel was satisfied that no drugs were on his person, nor in the Malibu he was driving. However, that was not the case.

"You can put your clothes on, dude," the cartel guy told him. "I can't say I'll be sorry to see that body of yours covered up."

"You're breaking my heart," the intruder replied. Once he finished putting on his shoes, the intruder said, "This has been fun, dude. I'll see you later."

"Not so fast, asshole," came the reply. "You're not going anywhere until I'm sure that all of the merchandise is here. So, sit your butt down on the bed while I count everything."

As the intruder sat there, he contemplated how easy it would be to punch out this guy's lights... permanently.

Meanwhile, the cartel guy considered texting his partner out in the parking lot with a message to put a bullet in the intruder's brain as soon as he exited the motel room.

It was after 1:00 p.m. by the time the cartel guy finished making a complete list of the drugs. At last, he was ready to allow the intruder to leave.

Before he did, he could not resist saying, "Take good care of Garrett's Malibu. You two will be switching the cars back next time we make a run. Whatever you do, don't do anything stupid while you're in his car. I'm sure you've been told, if you get caught, it will be your problem. Remember, if the cops don't catch you, we will... we know who you are and exactly where to find you."

"I've got it. Now can I leave already?" While the intruder continued to complain, he never let on that there was a dead body in the men's room at the Cog Railway Station. "This has turned into a bitch of a day. I can't wait to get home and put my feet up."

The cartel guy was quick to respond. "Did you say home? You're not going home, doofus. We can't have you doing that for at least a few days." Handing the intruder a slip of paper, he continued, "You'll drive from here directly to a safe house we've set up in Wolfeboro. Memorize the address, then give me back the piece of paper. Make sure you go right there... no detours... got it?"

Once the intruder assured the cartel guy that he would do as told, he received permission to leave. Feeling like he'd just escaped the confines of a pressure cooker, the intruder quickly put the Malibu into drive mode and turned left, heading south on Route 16.

❋ ❋ ❋ ❋ ❋ ❋

Kary later admitted to Director Williams that, as they landed at the hospital, he had no idea where their pursuit of the intruder would be taking them. Confusion turned to excitement moments later when Williams was patched through to Kary on the radio inside the state police car that met them.

"I take it you are all in North Conway," Williams said.

"We're all here," Norton replied.

"I have some news for you," came Williams reply.

"I know that tone, sir," Bendix said. "This is your 'terrific news' voice."

"It is indeed," Williams replied. "However, what I'd like you all to do is stay in the car and head south immediately. The trooper at the wheel knows where you're going. I'll fill all of you in during transit."

As Williams instructed, they sat in the back of the police car waiting for the director's news.

"Okay, first of all, we got a positive match on both the second set of finger prints from Dean's glasses and the image from the base station video."

"That Kairos Human Analytics program is amazing," Bendix replied.

"So, who are we looking for, Director?" Norton asked.

"This guy is a nasty customer. His name is Frederic

Close; he answers to the nickname "Claws." Close has a rap sheet as long as your arm. He's done time for robbery, several assaults, and is on the run from the authorities in Georgia."

"This is good information, Director," Kary told Williams. "However, he still has at least a half hour head start on us. Unless you have more information, he has a huge time advantage."

"I was just getting to that," Williams replied. Kary and the others could practically hear the smile in the director's voice. "It seems that the drug enforcement people in Quebec had been tired of tailing Garrett to the border only to lose him on this side. So, they asked the Sûreté du Québec to place a GPS tracking device on Garrett's car. Then, unfortunately, they got busy working on a bad traffic accident and stopped monitoring it right after Garrett parked his car at Glen."

"What caused them to resume monitoring the GPS in Garrett's car?" Kary asked.

"Dumb luck. About a half hour ago, one of their IT guys was looking for another car they were tailing, when he noticed that the Malibu had started moving again. That's when they contacted me."

It took Norton a moment to catch onto the meaning of what Williams was telling them. "But, Garrett's at Beecher Falls right now."

"That's right, Sergeant. He's sitting there in the murderer's car," Williams replied over the radio. "Our murderer has been driving Garrett's car…"

Norton completed Williams' sentence, "…which is being tracked!" Norton let out a whoop.

Williams said to Bendix, "The officer who is driving you has the necessary equipment to track Close from there. We'll let him do that, but first he's going to drop you three off at the Green Granite Inn. You'll rendezvous in the parking lot at 1400, just out of sight from room number ten."

"What's the significance of room ten?" Kary asked.

Williams replied, "Close's car was parked just outside of that unit for over an hour. We contacted the general manager of the inn, and he informed us that two men stayed in room ten last night. Both of them arrived in a car with Massachusetts plates and signed in under the name of Smith."

"That's not too suspicious," Norton laughed.

As they neared the inn, Williams spoke once again over the radio to Kary and Bendix, "Both of you will remain at the rendezvous point, please." Then Williams addressed Norton, "Sergeant, this part of the operation calls for your special set of skills."

For one of the few times that day, Norton's tone was very serious. "I understand, Director." However, the smile on his face indicated that he was relishing what came next.

"The troopers on the scene will have a Kevlar vest and gloves, and a helmet with a bullet-proof shield for you, Sergeant. Be certain you are wearing them when you enter room ten," Williams told him.

As they drove to the rear of the inn, Williams gave Norton one additional order, "We need these two people alive, Sergeant. They may know where Close is headed, just in case the GPS system gives out."

Chapter 15

After donning full armor, Norton and two other DTF officers quietly walked along the exterior of the Green Granite Inn. It was 1430. As this was a time of day that was an hour after check-out and two hours before check-in, it had been relatively easy to clear the housekeeping staff and any remaining guests away from the immediate vicinity.

At Norton's signal, one of the two troopers called out, "Armed State Police." Norton couldn't resist smiling. Clearly that officer had been watching British mysteries.

Having issued his warning, the trooper used a Dynamic Twin Turbo battering ram to burst open the locked door. Their entry took both members of the cartel by surprise. So quick was the team's access that neither man had the opportunity to reach for his Glock. The cartel member who had been giving Close so much verbal abuse decided to rush the officers and flee the premises. It proved to be an unfortunate decision. Norton acted so fast that the criminal never knew what hit him. Once he regained consciousness, he viewed a large officer looming over him.

Once the two men were of no danger to anyone, Norton texted Kary and Bendix, asking them to join him in the motel room. The badge Kary wore identified him as Commissioner for Visitor Safety for the State of New Hampshire.

The second member of the cartel, who said his name was Gil, found something humorous.

"Visitor Safety," he guffawed, "that's a hot one, huh, Lou. Isn't that sweet that this state pays people to wipe the arses and noses of a bunch of tourists."

Lou, the apparent leader of the pair, found his partner's comment funny.

"Yeah, that's a laugh all right, Gil."

Kary, as was his habit, remained cool under the circumstances. Moreover, unlike some previous cases where his personal safety was at risk, Kary felt secure knowing that Sergeant Norton had his back.

"I'm glad you find all of this funny. If I were found sitting in a room with tens of thousands of dollars in illegal drugs, I'm not sure I could find my situation quite so funny. You're both to be congratulated," Kary said in an obvious effort at sarcasm.

Suddenly, Lou was no longer seeing the humor in their situation. He made a move to rise, only to have Norton kick him just hard enough behind the knees to rethink the idea.

"Okay, okay. Tell me what you want. Only, keep this big gorilla of yours away from me."

"That sounds fair, Lou…is it all right if I call you Lou? You can call me Kary, if it makes you feel any better."

Nodding in the direction of Bendix, Kary told the two men, "I have several things to talk with you about, but first, Lieutenant Bendix here wants to have a chat about the drugs in your duffel bags. Looking at Bendix, he said,

"Please go first, Lieutenant."

"Thank you, Commissioner." Now, focusing her piercing gray eyes on the two men, she said, "Suppose you save me some time and effort. Why don't we begin by you telling me what the street value of those drugs is. Second, I want to know what the specific content of those duffels is." Next, forcing a wry smile she added, "I want to know where those drugs come from and the names of the people who procure and deliver them."

Lou let out a howl. "Oh, would you now, little missy? And, I'd like the numbers of the nuclear codes for the red phone in Washington."

Now it was Gil's turn to react. "Lou and me ain't telling you squat. You can count the drugs and figure out what their value is. And, we sure as hell aren't telling you the names of our bosses. We'll take jail over what those guys will do to us and our families if we rat them out."

Kary did not respond to the two men directly. Instead, he made a show of reaching into his pocket and removing his iPhone. Next, he hit speed dial and waited for the person on the other end to answer.

"Director Williams? Yes, this is Commissioner Turnell. Please instruct your officers to pick up Ned Garrett at Beecher Falls. And be certain to have them impound Garrett's white Chevy Malibu." After saying that, Kary closed the connection.

Down in Concord, Director Bill Williams sat at his desk smiling. Kary and Lieutenant Hollister had already informed him about the situation at the border. Garrett had been apprehended without resistance fifteen minutes earlier. It had been necessary to awaken him from his nap.

Using the office intercom to speak with his longtime associate, Williams said, "You were right about Kary Turnell, Simone. That guy is a real pistol."

The leader of the two, the man who identified himself as Lou, dropped his air of cockiness. The expression on his face was akin to someone who accidentally swallowed a housefly.

As usual, Norton couldn't resist remarking about the cartel member's change of demeanor.

"You're being awfully quiet, Lou," Norton chided. "You aren't blowing off very much steam right now. Is either of you rethinking your stance on talking to us?" He continued, "You boys have been caught red-handed with the goods. I'm sure the folks down in Concord will be more than happy to strike a deal with the first one who talks to us."

Bendix looked up from her laptop and nodded her agreement with Norton's proposal.

It was Gil who spoke first. Looking at Kary, he asked, "How did you cops know about Garrett?"

Before Kary could reply, Lou screamed at Gil, "Shut the hell up, Gil. If you open your mouth again, I'll personally make certain you're really, really sorry."

Next, looking at Kary, Lou asked, "Why the hell is the Commissioner for Visitor Safety on our case. Aren't you supposed to be out bandaging the knees of wounded tourists?"

"That line isn't very original, Lou," Kary replied calmly. He learned years before never to let a perpetrator see that he was annoyed. Deep inside, however, Kary was fighting to control his nerves and his anger. He decided to change tactics with these two men.

"Whoever came up with the idea to have identical cars on either side of the mountain was very clever. Was that your idea, Lou?"

Suddenly Gil laughed aloud. "His idea? Are you kidding? That came from our . . ."

Lou flashed his temper at the other man. "Keep your stupid mouth shut, Gil. I ain't gonna tell you again!"

Kary ignored Lou's outburst. Focusing his gaze solely on Gil, he continued. "Yes, that was very clever because anyone who was suspicious of Garrett would never guess that he had crossed over to the other side of Mt. Washington. They would never think that he already dropped off his drugs and was carrying cash back to Quebec."

"You just keep right on talking, mister. We ain't saying nothing," Gil replied.

Kary forced himself to maintain a confident air as he talked to the two men.

"Oh, I'm not so sure, Gil. When I tell you about your friend Mr. Close, you may have a change of heart."

"Who's Mr. Close?" Gil asked. Lou attempted a subtle wink at his partner, but Kary and Bendix saw it.

Norton quickly said to the two men, "Oh, that's right, you cartel people don't use real names when you're spreading your disease all over New Hampshire."

"But they both know who Garrett is," Bendix offered. "I saw the way they looked at each other when you mentioned his name, Commissioner."

"I saw that, too, Sergeant. And, something tells me that Garrett is going to be much more forthcoming than these two gentlemen… especially after we tell him about his friend Close."

Gil laughed, "Garrett doesn't know Close's name."

Lou growled at his partner, "Gil, shut your trap!"

Kary felt that this was a good time to play his trump card.

"I'm going to give you one last chance to talk to us, gentlemen. You two could get off with a comparatively light sentence if you help the lieutenant and the sergeant find your source. However, unless you do that right here and now, the charges I bring against you will place both of you in Concord prison until you're eligible for social security."

Gil said derisively, "What charges are you talkin' about, Mr. Visitor Safety?" He laughed at his own cleverness.

"I'm talking about your roles as accessories to murder," Kary said calmly.

"Murder?" Lou asked animatedly. "We didn't have nothing to do with no murder. Shoot, you're making that up. We may not be the most educated guys, but Gil and me ain't stupid."

"The Commissioner is telling you the truth," Bendix assured them. "Your man Close killed a seventy-four-year-old man at the Cog Base Station early this morning."

"I don't believe you. Why would Close do that?" Lou asked.

Kary knew that his best chance to gain the confidence of at least one of the men was by providing details of the incident. Neither Lou nor Gil moved so much as a finger while Kary described what he and the DTF knew about the cartel's efforts that morning.

For the next ten minutes, Kary briefly outlined what had transpired on Mt. Washington. He began by describing Garrett's drive from Quebec City, crossing the border at Beecher Falls, Vermont, before making a brief overnight stop at a small motor court on Route 2 in Randolph, a fact the investigative team had just learned. Kary then described how Garrett left his car in the auto road parking lot and rode a Mount Washington Stage van to the summit.

"I'm fairly certain you both know what happened next," he told the two men. Both sat staring at Kary without saying anything.

Kary told the men what DTF and his office learned, that Close had arrived at the Cog Base Station and desperately sought a ticket on the early morning steam train. When he found out that there was no ticket to be had, he looked at the passengers waiting on the platform.

"Arnold Dean must have stood out as a likely candidate. After all, he was seventy-four years old, looked older, and was traveling alone. Dean probably would have been fine except he needed to use the men's room at the last minute," Kary told them. "That's when your good buddy Close tailed Arnold Dean, took his ticket and killed him."

"Close wouldn't do that on purpose," Gil blurted out. "He ain't that kind of guy. It must have been an accident."

When Gil finished talking, he looked over at Lou who sat there shaking his head. Gil heard Lou call him an idiot under his breath.

Kary continued by telling the two men how Garrett and Close rendezvoused at the entryway to the Sherman Adams building on the summit. There was a very brief moment when the two were spotted together on closed CCTV. Both men were dressed similarly. From there, Kary told them, they walked, one at a time, into the Tip Top House. It was inside the Tip Top House's bunkroom where they exchanged their backpacks, caps, tickets and car keys surreptitiously, before switching places.

"Garrett took the Cog down to the Base Station and drove Close's car away. Close took the Stage van to Glen and took Garrett's car to meet you two."

Kary waited to allow everything to sink in for Lou and Gil. After a moment passed without either man saying anything, Kary told them, "This is your last chance, gentlemen. If you tell my colleagues what they want to know about your cartel, I promise not to charge you as accessories to murder."

Gil looked tempted, but a fierce look from Lou was all

the reason he needed to remain silent.

"That's a shame, gentlemen. I was trying to give you a break. But, I don't need information from you at all."

"You don't?" Gil whimpered.

Norton's patience had run out.

"No, we don't, you pathetic piece of garbage," he snarled. "It seems our counterparts in Quebec have been watching Ned Garrett for quite some time. Just like we have. The cops north of the border are pretty sophisticated. You see, they planted a GPS tracking device on Garrett's car two nights ago."

"Shit," Lou was heard to mutter.

"Shit happens, my man," Norton replied.

Kary told Lou and Gil that the ATF and DTF had trailed Close to a nice little house on Pine Street in Wolfeboro.

Gil made a move toward Lou but was quickly restrained by Norton.

"Close wanted to go home, genius!" Gil shouted at Lou. "But you're so damned clever, you just had to send him to the safe house. The whole operation's screwed!"

Norton couldn't resist chiding him. "See there, Gil, you could have been a hero. Now you're going to do major time just like the rest of your miserable cartel."

Chapter 16

To the collective disappointment of Kary, Bendix and Norton, they were still wrapping things up at the Green Granite Inn when, forty miles away, the action began in Wolfeboro. It was an hour before sunset when combined forces of the ATF, DTF and Wolfeboro police detectives surrounded a small cape with dark shingles at the east end of Pine Street.

Bill Williams arrived from Concord with a warrant, ready to lead the quickly but carefully planned onslaught.

Using a portable public address system, Williams called to the occupants of the house, "Frederic Close, we know you are in there. You and your friends need to put your weapons on the ground and walk out the front door with your hands raised. Any effort to lower your hands or to run from the scene will be interpreted as resisting arrest. You will pay the consequences of such actions." When his statement was met by silence, he ordered, "Everyone come outside right now!"

As three members of the cartel followed Williams' instructions and exited through the front door, Close used that distraction to cover his attempt to escape through a basement window. It was an ill-conceived idea that resulted in Close being wounded in his right thigh by a local detective's bullet. He was subsequently captured and handcuffed, and Miranda rights were read to all four. Then the three others were loaded into state police vehicles for transport to Concord. Close was treated for a flesh wound at the Huggins Hospital in Wolfeboro, then transported to Concord for arraignment before the state superior court.

※ ※ ※ ※ ※ ※

Owing to Frederic Close's heinous act, the state's newest drug cartel suffered irreparable damage. The cartel had prepared a clever plan to evade discovery and capture by directing its principal drug mule, Ned Garrett, to carry drugs from Quebec City to Glen, New Hampshire. From there, the drugs were transported to the summit of Mt. Washington, where a drugs-for-money exchange was carried out, away from public scrutiny.

Unbeknownst to Garrett and other members of the cartel, when Frederic Close arrived at the Cog Base Station and was unable to procure a ticket on the first coach to the summit, he reverted to past behavior. Quick collaborative action by DTF and Visitor Safety, aided by their Sûreté du Québec counterparts, with further support from ATF and the Wolfeboro police, brought about the swift arrests of Close and four of his cartel associates.

Meanwhile, as an effect of Kary's relentless pursuit of a murderer, the cartel suffered both a dramatic financial loss and a blow to their credibility as a drug supplier.

Once the order was given to capture Ned Garrett, there

was no place for him to run. Canadian border authorities had stalled his entry into Quebec province. When the order came to arrest the drug mule, New Hampshire and Vermont state police worked together to facilitate his capture.

When DTF searched the trunk of the Malibu that Garrett was driving, a cleverly disguised safe was found. Welded inside what appeared to be the car's spare tire was a reinforced steel cash box. The police immediately impounded the Malibu and, upon opening it, found more than $1 million in United States currency.

Meanwhile, the raids on the room at the Green Granite Inn and the house on Pine Street in Wolfeboro struck the motherlode. The combined haul at the two sites included ten kilos of cocaine, five kilograms of processed street methadone, five kilograms of heroin and five thousand Oxycontin tablets.

In the past, law enforcement in New Hampshire lost cases where clever legal representatives found holes in the state's evidence. Such was not the case in this instance. Kary and his DTF colleagues worked closely with the state's Major Crimes Unit to collect and properly tag physical evidence, procure electronic evidence from both sides of the international border, and obtain numerous eyewitness statements.

Both Close and Garrett had failed to heed the warnings of the cartel to be as invisible as possible. The sworn testimony of the Johnsons as well as the older woman, bearded man and driver at the Stage, when supported by evidence given by the ticket manager, marketing manager and brakeman at the Cog, and reinforced by employees at Fabyan's and the two border guards at Beecher Falls, was sufficient to positively identify both Close and Garrett. The jury found the evidence irrefutable, prompting the trial judge to congratulate the investigative work of Kary, Williams and the others.

The ramifications from the cartel's substantial loss of cash and illegal substances were felt throughout the drug world. Thus, New Hampshire's newest cartel was finished. Unfortunately, within several months, its place was taken by a new cartel that soon was preying on luckless drug-addicted citizens within northern New England.

※ ※ ※ ※ ※ ※

Frederic Close was charged with second-degree murder and one count of drug trafficking. Following his conviction, he began serving his life sentence in the New Hampshire State Prison for Men in Concord. Were it feasible for Close and Ned Garrett to visit one another, neither would need to travel very far. Garrett, Lou, Gil and the three men captured in Wolfeboro were each given forty-year sentences, also to be served in Concord.

Chapter 17

Kary's initial venture as Commissioner of Visitor Safety proved successful. Moreover, he found working with experienced DTF people, such as Williams, Bendix and Norton to be extremely fulfilling.

Governor David Steele was in office for five months when Close, Garrett, and the others were captured and arraigned. Needless to say, up until that point, Steele was under pressure from the public and the media for a lack of success in dealing with New Hampshire's number one social issue—substance abuse.

Naturally, Steele was overjoyed about the recent turn of events, and was determined to find a way to take political advantage of it. During a meeting with his press secretary, the two men thought of Kary.

When Kary heard Steele's voice on the phone, he was pleased to receive the governor's praise. That was before the governor informed him about a press conference where the focus would be on Kary's actions.

"We're calling you the 'twenty-four hour man,'" Steele told him. Hell, you got more results in a single day than DTF and our other law enforcement agencies achieved over several years. I want the public to be aware of what you've accomplished."

Kary's knew that the intended press conference was not really about him, and did his best to dissuade the governor. However, Steele informed Kary the press conference had been called for the noon hour that same day.

"I expect you to have a prepared statement, and be ready to answer questions," Steele told him.

As he hung up the phone, Kary felt like a man caught between a rock and a hard place. Naturally, the first person he contacted was his wife Nya, the person whose opinion Kary valued ahead of all others.

"This is a tough one, sweetheart," she replied to his explanation of the situation. "I don't know much about Concord politics, but I think you know someone who does." The idea came to Kary just as Nya said that.

"Bill Williams!" Kary exclaimed. "My love, you're a genius."

One short telephone conversation was all it took to bring Williams down the hall to Kary's office.

Kary shared what the governor had asked him to do.

Williams shook his head. "This could be a real opportunity for you, Kary."

"It also could produce an untenable situation for this task force," Kary replied.

The two men discussed the pros and cons of doing the governor's bidding.

"This would give you a lot of political clout with Steele. He'd owe you big time. If you want to pick your own full-time task force, it will happen. If you want your own helicopter... it's done," he added with a laugh.

"Some of that may be true, but any success I've had as an investigator in the past, or hope to have in the future, is based on sharing trust and respect with law enforcement personnel."

"One of the things I like about you, Kary, is you don't forget about the people who have made your success possible. With all you've accomplished, you could be a real egotistical asshole... but, that's not you... not at all."

Kary thanked Williams for his compliment, before continuing. "Can you imagine how people like Bendix, Norton and Hollister would react if I were to accept sole credit for our operation?"

Williams shook his head. "You know the answer to that question, Kary. But, I'm not going to tell you what to do because it's hard to predict how Steele will react."

※ ※ ※ ※ ※ ※

Every state news outlet, from traditional television, radio, and newspaper, to online news sites to political bloggers, was represented in the governor's conference room. Governor Steele began by providing a number of facts about drug abuse in New Hampshire, then reminded the media what they had been saying about his administration's weak response to the drug epidemic. Next, Steele reminded those assembled how the Major Crime Unit, DTF, and Visitor Safety had cooperated with other agencies to make a significant series of arrests. He gave Williams credit for his role in the operation, before turning to Kary.

"Many of you are familiar with the commissioner of my Task Force for Visitor Safety, Dr. Kary Turnell. Attracting Dr. Turnell to my administration was a real coup. His background in criminal investigation is without parallel. Up until now, I've been calling Kary, 'commissioner.' But, after his recent success, we are referring to him at the capitol as the 'twenty-four hour man.'" Steel then beckoned Kary to step forward and talk to the media.

Kary looked out into the audience. In the back of the room, he spotted Nya. Her presence provided all the incentive Kary needed.

"Ladies and gentlemen, I am most appreciative of the governor's expression of confidence. However, I want to make it clear that I'm no 'twenty-four hour man.'" As Kary said this, he looked at Steele out of the corner of his eye. The governor did not look pleased.

Kary continued, "With all due respect to Governor Steele, what happened up north was the culmination of the long-term determination of hundreds of dedicated career law enforcement personnel. It was simply coincidence that things came to fruition at the beginning of my tenure as commissioner. I deeply hope that officers Williams, Bendix, Hollister, Norton, Robison and the others who participated in this operation, found my contribution to their brave efforts to be of value. I'm honored to have worked alongside these talented, courageous people, and hope to have the opportunity to do so again."

Kary paused to give everyone a moment to absorb what he had said, before concluding, "I can promise you that we will make a constant effort to pursue, capture and punish perpetrators of criminal acts within New Hampshire's borders. My job as commissioner is to protect visitors to this state. However, no one who attempts to undermine the welfare of our citizens will escape our constant vigilance. Thank you."

The response to Kary's speech was very positive. Although Steele would have preferred for Kary to follow his script, the governor had to admit to his staff that the effect was satisfactory. For a short time, the media would cut Steele some slack about the drug issue.

※ ※ ※ ※ ※ ※

Two weeks later, Kary looked up from a stack of paperwork to see Bill Williams standing in the doorway to his office.

"Bill, this is an unexpected surprise," Kary said while offering the DTF director a chair.

"I'm here with news," Williams replied while eschewing Kary's offer to sit down. Seeing the look of anticipation on Kary's face, the DTF director did not mince words. "I have some good news, and one item of bad news to share."

Kary sighed. "Let's start with some good news."

"The good news is that both Bendix and Norton found working with you to be one of the highlights of their careers. Both were impressed with your ability to think on your feet, to make quick and accurate decisions, and to be decisive. I must say that I agree wholeheartedly on all fronts." Next, he added. "Also, every law enforcement official I've spoken with appreciated your comments at the governor's press conference. They realize that you were taking a real risk."

Kary's insight told him that Williams' next piece of news wasn't going to please him. "I presume that the bad news is there was no support for transferring Bendix and Norton to my task force, as I requested and you advocated," Kary said.

"Your powers of deduction are unassailable, Kary. However, in this case, you're only partially correct."

Kary looked confused, so Williams continued.

"I know that you were hoping to have Bendix and Norton join your unit immediately. Unfortunately, people who are considerably over my pay grade believe that they need to remain in the DTF."

"I should have expected that," Kary replied, while making no effort to disguise his disappointment.

"True, but that isn't the end of things," Williams said. "Bendix's three-year stint in DTF ends next month. She's requested to be transferred to Visitor Safety after her term. It's no sure thing but, after what's been accomplished, I think the chances are pretty good."

Kary forced a smile. "I suppose this represents progress," he said.

"It does," Williams replied. "And Norton probably won't